Malli

So nice to
talk with you
and laugh.

Aloha
Greg
Anthony
08

ZEN

AND THE ART OF SURFING

GREG GUTIERREZ

A COLLECTION OF SHORT STORIES

Zen and the Art of Surfing was published through a grant from the Julian Paz Foundation.

Zen and the Art of Surfing
Copyright © 2008 by Greg Gutierrez
Senior Editor: Dawn Pope
Assistant Editor: Dan Cain
Technical Advisor: Kathleen Brookes
Librarian Advisor: Kaight Taylor - She's an angel now
New Jersey Surfer Girl: Kelly Grace Thomas
Not so gentle reader: Paul Gallegos
Consultant: Chris Bradley
Available at Amazon.com
Eighth Printing

ISBN #1-59872-255-7

Registered Library of Congress
TX 6-329-668

Printed in America

Front and back cover: Delino Design
Author's photo: Renee Hindman Photography
Cover Painting by Greg Gutierrez - photographed by
The Surfer's Journal

This book is dedicated to my brother, Earl, who walks alone, humming an unknown song.

On July 23, 1988, my brother's boat, the Aita Pea Pea, was found adrift by the U.S. Navy. Earl Gutierrez was on his way home from a twelve-year, single-handed sail around the world. I visited with him just before he set sail from Honolulu to Los Angeles. It was with great emotion that he explained he was not ready to live in society's world. I wasn't sure what he meant then, and I'm not sure now.

Missing from his boat was his beloved bird, Pedro, and Pedro's large cage. Also missing were his passport and all his other personal belongings. There was no sign of foul play. The life raft was with the boat, but his handgun was missing. I believe he's out there somewhere, living under his own rules, as some men must do. The message I wish to send him is simple: I miss you.

An earlier version of *Zen and the Art of Surfing* was originally my Master's Thesis at San Diego State University. Excerpts of the collection have been published in *The Surfer's Journal*, *SURFER magazine*, *Surfing magazine,* and *Wave Action magazine*. Though many people helped me with this work, all of the mistakes are mine.

-Greg Gutierrez 2008

Contents

I Still Would

When I was four or five years old, I got into a fight with a bigger boy named Brian who lived next door. He took a barracuda jig that my Dad had bought for me. My Dad would bring us home something special when we were sick, and the barracuda jig was one of those gifts. I told Brian to give it back, but he just started walking away with it. I jumped on his back, and we fell to the ground. He ended up on top of me, swinging wildly. I was so mad that my already swelling eyes didn't hurt. Then my big brother was there, yelling at me to punch him in the face. So I did. As hard as I could until, bleeding, he ran home crying. My brother was laughing and telling me what a great fight it was. I had Brian's blood on my hands and my brother told me to be careful not to get any on his new Dale Velzy t-shirt.

When we got into the house I felt terrible. The feeling inside me was so ugly, so dirty. I started crying and my brother grabbed my face and looked into my eyes.

He said, "Don't cry. You won. Don't cry if you want to be my brother." I stopped crying. Later I went over the wall at the end of our street and cried some more.

Zen 1

That day I learned three things: I could take a punch, I could inflict pain, and though I wasn't supposed to cry, I still would.

That Sweet Smell

I broke into my first house when I was six years old. A kid at school was selling a new wax especially for surfboards. It smelled so good. It cost thirty cents a bar and my funds were nonexistent. So when Duke told us he knew where there was a jar full of dimes, we listened. By we, I mean me, and my then best friend, Oakey. He was lucky. His mom didn't make him bathe. Some guys had it made.

Duke was an unstable kid. He was a few years older but much tougher. He had to take some pill everyday to calm him down. Every once in awhile he'd forget his pill and beat the snot out of some unfortunate soul. On this particular day Duke seemed like he had taken his pill.

The house was across the street from Oakey's. We went into the backyard. Oakey knew the dog, so the dog stayed quiet. Duke lifted the sliding glass door and opened up the house. The jar of dimes was right out there on the counter for the world to see. Duke grabbed the jar, and then we hit the kitchen for some cookies.

We went to Oakey's house to divide the loot. Nobody was ever home at Oakey's. Naturally Duke got the lion's share. We made out pretty good, though. Oakey and I got five dollars and thirty cents each. In our world, that was some real money.

We spent some of our riches at Seaside Liquor. We bought candy, soda, chips, and other essentials. I saved some of my cash for the kid at school who was selling surfboard wax.

That night there was a knock on our door. Two tall policemen stood on our porch, and they wanted to talk to my Dad and me. One of the policemen just straight up asked me what happened. All three grownups were looking at me.

I told them, "Duke made us do it. He said he'd beat us up if we didn't go with him. That's the truth. Everyone knows that Duke's crazy. I'm afraid of him."

The same cop said to my dad, "Yeah, that's what the kid named Oakey said. Given what I've heard about Duke, I'm inclined to believe your son here. Sorry to have bothered you, have a good night."

When we got into the house my Dad quietly told me, "I never want to see the police on our front porch looking for you again. Do you understand?" I did, and I learned something that day - *don't get caught.*

I bought four bars of wax the next morning at school. If I try, I can still remember that sweet smell.

Earn It: February 2007

I was surfing a far away place, being held under so long that my arms and legs were numb. I felt a ragged part of my board jabbing at my neck. I tried to shield myself but my arms felt as if they were tied down. Again and again my board stabbed at my Adam's apple. *"Christ, he's turning blue, intubation is a no-go; he's closed. I can't even get a pediatric size down. We're losing him, let's cut."*

And my Rusty pierced through my throat and darkness rushed in from all sides as I fell into the abyss.

Then I was body surfing Sandy Beach with one of my students, Kealoha-Pauole Lomu, a relative of Eddie Aikau. We laughed and glided through the aqua power, the warm water propelling us through section after section.

I dreamt I was tied on a hospital bed, a contraption coming out of my throat, both arms streaming with numerous tubes, Robocop-like machines wrapped around each leg, pulsating with a mechanical rhythm. I tried to control my dream as I have done so many times; willing filet knives into each hand so I might cut the binding cords, but the blades would not appear. Like an animal I fought the constraints and the voices of spirits slipped in.

A man asked "Is he on anti-depressants?"

My wife's lovely voice replied, "No, he's the mellowest person you'll ever meet."

A different man said, "Let's tighten him up, he's breaking free."

My wife whispered, "I can't see him like this."

Late that night I reached for a pad of paper and wrote a note to the nurse, *"I want to hear my wife's voice, please call her."*

She put the phone to my ear and my best friend said, "I love you honey, I'll be there at first light. Try to sleep now Beanie, good night." I was then able to find some fitful rest.

I woke up with a start because I couldn't breathe. A kind, tiny Indian nurse rushed to me and pulled a tube out of my throat, saying, "Cough!" I did and I was able to fill my lungs. I lingered on the edge in intensive care. I heard the words, "critical, tracheotomy, epiglottitis, low platelet count, aggressive streptococcus and walled pneumonia." The morphine dripped and dripped.

In eight days I lost thirty-five pounds. The doctors told me I probably should have died but I never thought I would, I love my precious wife and kids too much for that. Besides, I had a Cub Scout campout at San Onofre with my son to go to. I needed to see my daughter who had the lead role in her school play. I had students to teach, the word of Christ to study, and waves to catch. The whole ordeal was a blessing; life tastes sweeter. I believe it all began while surfing filthy, stinky, Cardiff Reef. Afterwards I went to my doctor with flu-like symptoms and he sent me home. That night I took an ambulance to a hospital but they didn't see anything serious. The next morning I went to a different hospital. I told the girl in emergency, "I can't breathe or swallow." She said, "You're standing there aren't you? So I guess you're breathing. You've got a drink in your hand, so I guess you're swallowing."

Luckily I was seen by an old doctor who looked like Mark Twain, he said, "There's a rare disease that you might have; let's X-ray your throat." They did so and afterwards the doctor rushed to me and said, "You've got it, let's go to the O.R." It's a miracle that this doctor recognized epiglottitis when other doctors didn't. My vocal chords are damaged and I talk like the Godfather. But the good Lord has given me another chance. Now I've got to earn it.

Maya
For Mark Foo

Originally published in *The Surfer's Journal*

The young man went to the ocean's edge and was saddened by its flatness. This was a time that the man physically needed to ride waves, yet the sea was calm. The waves were all things to him. He sat down to eat his meal of sticky rice. An old, thin man wearing only a white wrap around his manhood, walked up to him.

The old man said that he was hungry and that he would like some rice.

The young one looked at the old man, and for reasons he did not understand, he said, "Please eat."

The old man ate the rice and said, "I would like to express my thanks for the rice by giving you some waves to ride."

The young man laughed and asked, "How?"

From a small, leather pouch he pulled out three wrinkled black and white photographs and said, "Choose one." One photo was of Tunnels, rights breaking, big and lined up forever. Another was of Windmills, Kona winds blowing and perfect swell direction. The last picture was of Wiamea Bay, so big that it did not look real.

The young man was skeptical but figured he had nothing to lose. He asked, "When?"

The old man said, "Get your board and sit in this triangle." He drew a triangle in the sand. The young man grabbed his board and sat in the triangle. The old man asked which picture he liked and the young one answered, "Tunnels."

"I like that one myself," the old man replied. "Now hold on tight to your board, look at the picture and say 'Maya.'"

As soon as the young one said the word, he was under water, holding on to his board with all his strength. He popped out of the sea and before him broke Tunnels, in all her glory. There was one other person out. He was very dark and rode a wooden board, which he glided through the long round bowls with ease. They did not speak, but rode the tunnels in silence. After five hours, the young man paddled outside the lineup and said, "Maya."

He was back on the beach next to the old man. Though he was exhausted, he knew that no time had passed. The old one said, "Bring some rice tomorrow and you can take another trip."

The next day the young man returned to the sea, the old one appeared.

"Where to today?"

"Windmills," replied the young one from inside the triangle. The wind began to blow out of the east, and the smell of California sage filled his lungs.

The old man pulled out the photograph and held it in front of the young one, who said the word, "Maya." Again he was under water, straining to hold on to his board. He surfaced and quickly started paddling towards a gaping lefthander. The wind howled straight offshore. There was no one in sight. The young one rode the waves for six hours, until his arms would no longer move. He paddled outside and said, "Maya."

Again he was next to the old one, and it seemed that no time had passed. The old one smiled and said, "See you tomorrow."

The next day the young one returned with his longest board.

He offered the bowl to the old man who said, "Today, you eat the rice."

The young one ate the rice, sat in the triangle and said, "Wiamea Bay."

The old man said, "Goodbye."

The young one, so full of life, whispered, "Maya." He did not return.

*To ride inside
the eye
is to hold the
golden lotus.*

09/13/21 5:27PM 1019   633   SALE

888641132393   -1 EA   7.99 EA   R
ZIG DOG ZIGGY BARS SALMON   -7.99
Orig: D01366/17 09/08/21 TX:

SUB-TOTAL:$ -7.99 TAX: $ -.62
                     TOTAL: $ -8.61
   REFUND: 8.61

==>> JRNL#D02421/17   <<==
       CUST NO:*17
          Customer Copy

___THANK YOU FOR SHOPPING AT KAHOOTS___

09/13/21 8:27PM 1019   633   SALE

9966411323393   -1 EA   7.99 EA   R
ZIG 00Z ZIGGY BARS SALMON   -7.99
Orig: D01266717 09/08/21 TX:

SUB-TOTAL: $ -7.99   Tax: $ -.62
            TOTAL: $ -8.61
   REFUND: 8.61

Fidel

Originally published in *The Surfer's Journal*

As a child I liked the way my sinuses tingled after I had gone swimming in the surf. I liked the way the water felt as it flowed through my system. As I grew older I began to try and breathe water – just a little. Today, I like to inhale the ocean. I think most of the water comes back through my mouth. Some is absorbed by my lungs. It's just something I've come to enjoy.

The winter of 95-96 has delivered. There hasn't been the consistency and size of 94-95, but there has been solid surf. One of my goals this winter has been to catch big Todos Santos as much as possible. Constant obstacles to Todos trips are finding people who want to go and who have the money. A few weeks ago the conditions were perfect. Mid-morning low tide, and Sean Collins was predicting quadruple-over head for Todos. No fog and clear skies. I picked up the phone and started making calls. I finally found a fellow teacher who agreed to go with me.

We both teach at a year-round school so we have a lot of weekday winter surf time. That night I could not sleep. I never can when the surf is big. I toss and turn and watch the alarm clock. At 3:00 a.m. I was up and making coffee. My friend called and said he had changed his mind - he just wasn't ready for it. I tried to talk him into making the journey, but he would not go. I tried to convince myself that La Jolla would be on fire, but I couldn't curb my disappointment.

My wife came downstairs and asked who had called.

Before I knew what I was doing I said, "Oh, it was just Jim. He wanted to make sure I didn't oversleep." That was it. I was going solo. I loaded up my truck with my two favorite guns and headed for the border.

After I bought my insurance I crossed into Mexico. Since I had surfboards, it was a given that I would go to Mexico's secondary border search. Whenever I tell Mexican police that I am a teacher, they always extend their courtesy. This time was no exception. I made it to San Miguel in an hour and a half. As I pulled off the highway in the early morning darkness, I could see white water sweeping across the break and into the bay. I didn't want to watch it for too long. I knew that if I did, I'd change my mind about Todos. I headed for Ensenada Harbor.

The first yellow light of day showed itself as I turned right into the parking lot. As usual, many men approached with variations of the same theme – a fast boat with a good captain. I already knew the captain I was looking for. Fidel. I've known Fidel for twenty-five years. He was a friend of my father's and knows his boat well. I found him and we agreed on sixty dollars since I told him we'd be back by noon. I loaded his rickety orange boat and we waited about fifteen minutes to see if any other surfers might show up. Being a weekday, that wasn't likely. Finally, we headed out as the sun warmed the morning air.

As soon as we got out of the harbor we were met with a ground swell that was thick and solid. The boat climbed the swells, in and out of the morning light. I could see huge whitewater on the mainland side of the island and Fidel must have sensed that I was nervous. He told me about a day he remembered when one wave broke three boards. He laughed and joked with me and told me about his family. I realized that this man (with brown, broken teeth) was living a life that was real and good. I was glad to be on his boat and to share my food with him.

The water at big Killers is a color I can barely comprehend. The light catches the wave where the lip throws and makes the blue-green waves light up brilliantly. As Fidel decided where to anchor, I watched the swells thunder into the bay from far out of the empty sea.

Thoughts flowed through my mind as I put on my wetsuit. "Earl, Earl, the black pearl, where are you, brother? You rode the ocean swells and I'm waiting for you. My wife, my life, do you know how you have made me complete? Baby girl, I simply love you. You are my heaven and joy. Where are you, father? Heaven or hell? Heaven, I pray…it's really good."

I kept repeating in my mind, "It's really good." I grabbed my 10'2" Surfer's Alliance and paddled for the outside. It was amazing how perfect the swells were: solid, consistent, clean, triple-over head waves, with a macking bigger wave every half hour, or so. I rode what felt good and avoided the mackers. The thing was, the mackers were perfect. I decided I needed to catch one.

Things felt perfect as I scratched over the edge of my biggest wave of the day. I started my turn early and angled down the face. The drop was gloriously long. My board knew exactly what to do. The section in front of me started to pitch, and I felt that my line was strong and open. I pulled in and for just a moment the world was balanced. That's when I made my mistake. Instead of focusing on my escape, I looked back into the soul of the wave. I must have hit a bump or something because the next thing I knew I was bouncing across the wave as the lip landed on top of me.

I'm not sure how long I was under. Way longer than I ever want to be under again. I tried to calm myself but it's tough when you're getting the crap beat out of you. When I finally surfaced, all that remained of my board was about eighteen inches of the tail section. I pulled the quick-release on my leash and tried to get my bearings. I had been tossed the length of the break and was about thirty yards from "the rock," which is the size of a VW bus and sits just inside the pit. I started stroking for the channel, but the waves kept pouring through. I was in trouble.

I really wasn't thinking about anything – just swimming hard and trying to get air. The water around me was so turbulent that it was difficult to breathe. I had trouble keeping my head up. The power of the ocean was overwhelming me, and I knew then that I could not breathe water.

I didn't see him until he was nearly on top of me. Fidel had charged into the surf in his beautiful orange boat. He swung it around and threw out a yellow line in one smooth motion. I grabbed the rope and he gunned his boat towards the channel. We made it out of the lineup, and he helped me on board. Then he looked me in the eye and laughed like hell. I laughed too.

Only the thing for which you have struggled will last.

-Yoruba proverb, Nigeria

The Haole

He was guilty of the gravest sin. It was unspoken, but his people had ruined the land. They took advantage of the innocence of an entire chain of islands. They tore down nature and built hotels. Hotels the natives would only enter to work in, never to enjoy.

An outsider, a drop of oil in a glass of water. A young man at the bottom of the food chain. One who walked with his head down at all times. He was not afraid; that's not why his head was down. He was just someplace else. He was mind surfing. A boy named Jordan who paid for the sins of the white man. A haole in Lahaina Luna High School.

He and his mother were new to the island. On his first night in Lahaina he saw something that shook him some place deep down inside. Lahaina was a town of whalers and pirates. Late at night, after the bars close, the Lahaina of yesterday sometimes comes alive. Jordan was awakened by the sound of a man in turmoil. He looked out the window of their Banyan Tree apartment. A battered haole limped down the street dragging a huge metal chain. His face had a long open cut across his cheek. His legs were bleeding and his shirt was nearly torn off. The chain clinked against the pot-holed street.

The limping haole was crying hysterically and babbling, "I'm gonna fuck him up, I'm gonna fuck him up." At first Jordan thought the babbling man was coming to his apartment, but the man just continued down the street, and into the night.

"Welcome to Maui," Jordan whispered to himself. He got the biggest kitchen knife and kept a lookout. His mother found him sleeping in the morning, by the window, with the knife in his hand.

Jordan and his mom had moved from Sunset Cliffs and were initially deceived by the island's beauty. She had raised Jordan by herself, and by most standards she did a damn fine job. But she was a woman in a land of men. On Jordan's first day as a freshman, he had his head slammed down on the desk so hard it broke his nose. He gave back, but he was not built to overcome the island's assortment of Hawaiians (if you fight one, you'll fight many), Tongans (slow to get mad, but unstoppable when started), Samoans (sheer size and strength), Filipinos (pound for pound a vicious fighter), and other members of the polyglot.

By the tenth grade people gave him a little more space but not because he could give back well (though he'd fight until he couldn't get up). It was because there was something Jordan could do as well as any Lahaina Luna boy. He could surf. Word got out that Jordan was a charger. He could surf Honolua Bay like a man. Subs, Coconuts, the Cave, it didn't matter. He charged. Yet he still was not allowed inside the circle of future watermen at Lahaina Luna. No, there was a line he could not cross. There was a difference that ran too deep. He would never date a beautiful island girl. He would never be asked into the warm and safe glow of an islander's friendship. No, Jordan's friend was the ocean. And it welcomed him like a lover.

One Christmas morning Honolua was huge and pristine. The boys of Lahaina Luna gathered at the boat launch well inside the bay. It was only there that one could safely paddle out on such a strong day. Jordan showed up and looked out upon the sea. "The Bay" was perfect, but there were no less than 100 people out. Then Jordan started looking at the left that came in south of the boat ramp. He had never seen or heard of anybody surfing the left. As the well overhead left broke, it raced across the rocky shoreline with speed and flirtatious danger. Jordan watched the wave and believed he could ride it.

Jordan knew all the Lahaina Luna boys would be watching him. He paddled out quickly before he changed his mind. He got in position and deftly took off left, not fifteen feet from the rocky shore. He pulled up as high as he could and screamed across the wave. The swell broke with speed and precision along the precarious shore. The wave threw itself out to the hungry rocks, and Jordan was dry reefed. Just like that, he went from wave to reef. Jordan took gas. He got rolled around the rocks and eventually came to a stop. As he limped back to the boat launch the Lahaina Luna boys were screaming with delight. God, how they enjoyed watching Jordan get pummeled.

As Jordan got closer, the boys could see a grin on his bloody face. The tone of the Lahaina boys seemed to soften. Then Jordan walked to the water's edge and paddled out for another go at the impossible left. The

Zen 19

Lahaina boys grew silent.

This time Jordan chose a different line. Instead of climbing high on the wave, he dropped halfway down the face. Jordan rode in the pit as the wave spun all around him. The wave broke faster, and Jordan made subtle adjustments that kept him in front of the churning foam ball. Then the wave spit out its energy, and Jordan emerged from the tube with a smile. He popped out the backside of the wave, and he heard the Lahaina boys scream his name.

Jordan got out of the water and thought maybe he was done for the day. Then one of the Lahaina boys said, "Dis place called Jordan's now. You like to go wit us to Rainbows, o wat?" And that's the day Jordan became a Lahaina Luna boy.

Ask and it shall be given you;
seek and ye shall find;
knock and it shall be opened
unto you.

-Matthew 7:7

Sunset Cliffs

Keone walked into his classroom on Monday morning toting his coffee and surfboard. The administration had gotten used to Keone always having his board around. His first period advisory class came in. There was Margarita, who was so poor she sometimes wore a pajama top to school. There was Trina, who was scared, because the man who molested her when she was very young just got out of jail and was hanging around where she lived. He wore a white baseball cap and white jacket. He just stared up into her second story apartment singing *Happy birthday to you.* Trina had lost her spunk and it stirred something in Keone's bones. Her mother had contacted the sheriff but the man in the white cap and jacket would just slip away before they arrived. He had violated his parole but they couldn't catch him, just one more scumbag scrambling around on the loose, wreaking havoc, fear, and pain on his way to death, or back to prison.

There was little Marky, whose big brother just got his head blown off by his supposed best friend. Marky's brother had broken into his grandfather's house and stolen a handgun. They played Russian roulette and Marky's brother lost.

For a moment Keone asked himself the same old questions, "Am I making a difference in these seventh graders' lives? Does what I do matter? Is my life worthy?" Then he looked into the eyes of the children and knew that this was the best possible thing he could do with his time on this planet. Yeah, there were better neighborhoods where he could teach, but there was no place he'd rather be.

He picked up the newspaper for it was current events day. For just a moment he lost his breath. There on the cover was the news that one of his favorite writers had died. What is it about children that give them a sixth sense about an adult's emotions? They could see their teacher was hurting.

Keone spoke, "A friend is dead." Keone wondered if he should go on about him, then decided that, yes, he would tell his story.

"About a year ago I got into a big fight with my wife. I wanted to go tuna fishing and she didn't think we could afford it. She was right, but that wasn't the point. Of course, I forgot what the point was. The albacore were literally jumping into boats. I was so mad that I slept in our guest room. I woke up early and read the newspaper. There was a long article written by a master writer. He wrote about how scared he was because he had brain cancer. He wrote about how he really loved Sunset Cliffs.

Zen 23

He told his readers about his fear of death. His words spoke right to me. See, kids, he could write. He could put the whole universe into one sentence. He just crawled right into my heart and sat down next to me. His voice seemed to be as familiar as an old friend. He wrote about how he longed to have a wife and children. It seemed like he wrote just for me.

"I went to my wife and daughter. I woke them up and held them close for a very long time. He had really opened my eyes. I had an art exhibit on Coronado Island at the time. One of my favorite paintings in the show was one titled, 'Sunset Cliffs.' I called the newspaper and told them that if the writer wanted the painting, it would be my pleasure to give it to him. The newspaper sent someone over to pick up the painting. It felt good to give the painting to him. I've been reading his words for the last year, and I'm feeling pretty sad."

Keone felt the tears welling up behind his eyes. This had happened before when a really bright young man had to leave the school. He just didn't have anyone that could take proper care of him, so he was sent to foster care. His grandfather had been collecting cans to support the boy, but he could no longer make ends meet. Keone asked his wife if they could adopt him. With tears in her eyes she held him close.

She looked at Keone and said, "You can't bring them home, honey, they're too many. If you're going to teach, you've got to realize that."

Before the student left he gave a quiet, lovely girl a red rose, then walked out the door. It was one of the most beautiful things Keone had ever seen. As he watched him walk away, tears came but he told the students he had something in his eye; he fooled them.

Then Keone remembered a professor he had at San Diego State. Once, while Dr. Jackson Benson was reading the end of Bernard Malamud's "The Magic Barrel," he started crying. Dr. Benson didn't even wipe his eyes, he just kept on reading, showing his students what great teaching looked like. Then Keone thought about the courage the writer had to share the experience of his own death. Keone let the tears come.

"I know you're only in seventh grade and it's hard to see your teacher cry, especially since I'm a man. But someone very good has died and it makes me very sad. It's okay to cry when you're sad." Tears fell from Keone's eyes. "You see, I don't quite understand why he's gone. I know there's a heaven, and I know he's there. Maybe he's watching us right now and smiling because he knows he made a difference. And it's a good thing, to make a difference."

That night Keone couldn't stop thinking about the courage it would take to write about one's own death. Then he started thinking about the molester who was stalking his student. He knew what he had to do to so that he could sleep at night.

He told his wife and daughter he was going for a night surf. This was not unusual. Night surfing was his escape. He liked to go later in the night when the moon was high. He wasn't going surfing though.

Around eleven o'clock that night he drove to the neighborhood of his student. Keone parked on a side street and grabbed his baseball bat from behind his seat. He quietly got out of the car and walked slowly to the corner of the apartment building. He peeked around.

There he was. The man was wearing a white baseball cap, a white jacket and singing his birthday song. Keone could see the molester's back.

His guess was that this creep was high as a cat's tail on something. He just peered up at Trina's window. Keone toyed with the thought of giving the twisted guy some sort of chance and making it some sort of fair fight. Then he thought better of it and came up behind him and swung with all his might. He remembered how Coach Rory taught him to hit. Choke up. Watch the target. Level elbow. Step into the swing. Follow through. Keone connected crisply with the back of the dirt bag's left knee. The sound was nice.

"Oh, that's a single."

The power of the swing swept *the man from glad* up and onto his back. He screamed pretty good and rolled into a ball trying to hold his knee.

His eyes were glassed over and he spit out, "You're dead! You're fucking dead." Keone went for his other knee. The man stupidly tried to protect it with his arms but that was a mistake. This time there were two loud snaps.

"That, my friend is a double."

Heightened primal screaming reminded Keone that he might want to hurry up. He swung on The Man from Glad's ankles. Two more solid whacks and Keone was done.

"Stand up triple and a homerun to boot. Bro, you really can't sing." Keone hustled back to his car, started driving, and didn't turn on his lights for a few blocks. A ways down the road he stopped at a pay phone and called the Sheriff.

He told the young woman who answered the call, "Send a unit to Canal Drive and Mango Street. There's someone you're looking for." Then he hung up.

The next day at school Trina had her old spunk back.

Like the moon
Come out from behind the
clouds!
Shine.

-The Buddha

The Animal

Originally published in *Wave Action magazine*

"Gather round this old man and let me bend your ear. You ain't seen nothing. Ain't seen a damned thing. Have you ever thought about killing a man? Yeah, taking some son of a bitch's life. I got over it. But there was a time when I thought the Animal would be better off dead. So much hatred inside the man. Yeah, I had it all planned out. It's kinda sad to look at him now. The Animal. He doesn't even surf anymore. He just looks through the trash for cans and bottles. He's afraid of his own shadow. He's afraid of voices from the sky. He's living in Hell now. Paying for the sins of his life.

"When the Animal was in his twenties he was truly an animal. The scum was just huge and hairy. He surfed dead winter L.P. Point without a wetsuit. No leg rope. He couldn't surf for shit but he never lost his board. He just sort of muscled it across the easy part of the best inside waves. He never ventured outside. No, that son of a bitch sat right on the boil and took off on everyone. While he paddled after the waves he'd be yelling, 'Come on mother fucker, come on mother fucker.' He would yell obscenities at the wave as he rode it in his coarse and ugly style. He'd scream, 'Come on whore, come on, let me ride you, let me ride you!' To surf with him was to have your mother ocean spit on, time and time again.

"I learned just to stay the hell away from him. He only surfed on the smaller days, the chicken shit. The thing about the L.P. crew was, in those days, they were the bottom of the barrel. Those boys weren't a blue-collar crowd; they were a no-collar crowd. They'd sit on the rocks around the corner from the stairs. Right below these three million dollar homes they had set up a rock fort. Sometimes some of them lived in it. Some of the sons of bitches didn't even surf. They'd just shoot their heroin and then raise hell with anyone who happened to come along. I surfed there. I just stayed clear of the Animal, and didn't get close enough to shore to get pegged by a rock. I used to paddle in from the park.

"One day this guy paddled out on an Old Local Motion gun. The guy was a small Oriental man who looked about forty or so. There was something about the Oriental man, you know, just as happy as a hillbilly. You could see by his quiet paddle that he was a waterman. So, anyway, he took off way back round the outside, trimming his gun up to speed, a joy to witness. I just had fun watching that little man fly.

"Sure enough, out paddles the Animal. His sidekicks weren't on the rocks this particular day; I reckon they were out robbing a house or something. He paddled right up to the little Oriental ripper and starting growling like a wild dog. 'Grrrrrrrrrrrrrrrrrrrroowl!' I didn't know what the hell was gonna go down cause I knew the little man was not your everyday hodaddy. Well, the little man looked right at the Animal and starting laughing like a son of a bitch. He just laughed this deep kinda crazy laugh and paddled back to the outside.

"Before long the little man was humming nicely from way outside up to the boil. Well, Animal sure enough took off and all be damned if the little man didn't shoot right by him! The Animal was so blown away that he fell right off his board and his shitty old stick got pummeled on the rocks. The little man just laughed and left the Animal screaming, 'Take it to the beach, take it to the beach, you little Jap fucker. Come on you little Jap fucker!' Well, the little man finished his wave and paddled out for another one. Meanwhile the Animal was swimming after his board screaming, 'Vengeance is mine!'

"By the time the Animal was back out in the lineup, the little man was cruising across a beauty. The Animal was caught a bit inside and the little man shot towards him at mach speed. You could hear the Animal shouting, 'I'm going to kill you.' While flying by the Animal, the little man yelled, 'Hey bra, more bettah you no get you panties all bunched up, eh?'

"We didn't know what was gonna happen, nobody had ever stood up to the Animal before. When the little man paddled by me, he said, 'Hey guy, dis big hoale come to me, I going pound him in kine sef defense, yeah? You witness fo me, or wat?' I told him, 'Oh yeah, I'll be your witness, but you better watch that guy.' The little man laughed his joyous laugh and went out for another wave. Meanwhile, the Animal was frantically screaming, 'Take it to the beach you little Jap fucker!'

"The little man smiled, and shouted back, 'All right den.' He paddled towards the rocky shore. Since I agreed to witness for the little man, I paddled in with him. The Animal's mistake was that he thought he was just going to destroy the little man.

"They got out of the water at the same time, about thirty yards from one another. The Animal threw his board down and charged the little man. The little man laughed his joyous laugh. Just before the Animal reached him he threw his board aside and in his hand held a rock the size of a cantaloupe. The Animal hesitated for just a second and during that second the little man hurled the rock at the Animal's stomach. It was a beautiful throw, just like a fast pitch softball player. The rock landed with a sickening crack, and the Animal fell straight to the ground. The little man then picked up the same rock and grabbed the Animal by the hair. The Animal looked bad, real bad; his eyes were crossing and he was foaming at the mouth. He pulled the Animal's face close and said, 'Next time dis rock go on you head, guy.' The Animal was never the same after that. I guess in some twisted way it's kind of sad. Naw."

It's an innocent trip
to paddle out
towards sensuous solitude

through the chaotic avalanches
away from mediocrity
further and further

my head now burns
for the hair leaves
yet the child lives

further still further
into the abyss
committed no less

torched arms
until God whispers
you are alive

The Trap

The storm's wind blew the leafless branches against the cracked window. Seven-year-old Chulo woke up to the smell of chorizo and eggs. He rose and bound his sleeping mat into a tight roll, as his mother liked it. His mother had left him four burritos for his breakfast. She had already left to clean the house of the others. He didn't know his father.

When he would ask about him, his pretty mother would reply, "The less said the better."

Being Saturday, Chulo did not have to go to school at Imperial Beach Elementary. He loved Saturdays above all other days. Sundays were okay, but he really didn't like having to stay awake during church. Chulo walked out of the two-room home into the cold, windy sunlight.

Zen 33

Chulo and his family lived in a house behind another house. Between the two small houses lived a man named Loveless. Loveless slept in a small wooden box that sat on four red bricks. He was a gringo with a long blond ponytail. He washed himself with the garden hose every morning. Loveless had been in prison and had many tattoos. The biggest said *Dago Bikers* across his chest. His body was hard and cut. Nobody fucked with Loveless. Today Loveless was making lobster traps out of wire.

"Loveless, why aren't you out fishing today?" asked Chulo.

"Hey, buenos dias, Chulo. It's too windy today. The lobster traps get blown all over the place in weather like this and it's hell in the boat."

"Yeah, too rough, huh? You want one of my burritos?"

"No. You eat them. Get some meat on your bones. I just had a big breakfast." Chulo looked around and knew that Loveless had not eaten anything.

"Loveless, my mom made two for you." It was true; his mother had begun to cook for Loveless and somehow that really pleased Chulo.

"Tell your mom thanks for me."

"You tell her yourself."

"I just might do that."

"Okay."

"Okay."

Loveless bent the large fence-like wire to form a wire box.

"Hey Loveless, why do the lobsters go into the trap?"

"Because they're hungry. They smell the fish I put into the trap and crawl through the small hole in the wire. When they're caught in the trap, they can't even eat the fish they smell because it's locked up tight. When the other lobsters see the trapped lobsters they think, 'Hey, there must be something good there, so I'm gonna go there too.' Before long, I got myself a trap full of lobsters that I can sell to the wholesalers for some pretty good bucks. I'm having a hell of a great season. I'm buying my own boat."

Chulo said, "Your own boat. Oh, Loveless, that's great! The lobsters remind me of my family. We came through a hole in the fence because it looked so good in this country, but it seems like the food is locked up pretty tight. We're as dumb as the lobsters."

"Naw, hungry like the lobsters, but smarter. Your mother brought you and your brother here because she knows there's a better chance for you on this side of the fence. You're very lucky to have such a mother; she's something else. I didn't know mine very well. Where's that brother of yours?"

"He didn't come home last night. But he must have been here this morning because his newspapers are gone. He's been away a lot. My mom says she's gonna send him to my tio's in Texas 'cause he ain't been too right."

Chulo's brother Ernesto was about to be jumped in to MBS - Mexican Boy Soldiers. Ernesto was not sure about being jumped in. He could either join them or fight them. There were just too many. He had told himself he'd join but continue to attend his classes. Ernesto had a paper route and the money he brought in made it just possible for the family to live in their two-room house.

Loveless said, "Well, some of his homies were here, stay away from them. Maybe later we'll go down to the ocean and you can try surfing my Skip Frye."

Chulo loved the ocean, the smells, sounds and waves. He would go whenever he could to watch the surfers from the pier. There were some crazies, druggies, thieves and bullies on the pier, sure, but he felt at home there. Sometimes he'd clean up around the restaurant for a little money or lunch.

Ernesto walked in from the alley. "Chulo," he hissed, "anybody been around?"

"Yeah, your punk friends," Loveless answered. "What's going on?"

In a soft voice Ernesto answered, "They went too far. They shot some fool just because he painted over their tag. I think they killed him. I'm out. I thought I was a killer, but I'm not! They don't trust me for shit, think I'm gonna talk. I'm no rat, but I'm gone."

Loveless took charge. "You get in your house. I'm gonna be around for awhile. They won't bother you as long as I'm around. When your mom gets home, she'll decide what to do."

Chulo was glad that Loveless was there to make things right. No one would cross Loveless, but he would not always be around.

When Chulo's mother came home that afternoon and learned that Ernesto was in trouble, she didn't hesitate. She knew what she had to do.

"Put your things into a box, you're going to your tío's. We'll buy you a ticket. Loveless will walk you to the bus station. Come on, hijo, you must be gone before it is dark."

Ernesto replied angrily, "Mama, we don't have the money for a bus ticket. Use your head; you can't spend the rent money, it's due tomorrow!" His mother slapped him hard across the face.

"Don't be disrespectful. Chulo and I will be fine. We have always been fine. I've got some pay coming for my cleaning and I'll collect what I can. Chulo can handle your newspapers. Now move."

Ernesto took Chulo into the other room. "Chulo, tomorrow is collection day for my paper route. You know the route. Here is the list of all the money that's due. After you deliver all of the Sunday papers, go back along the route and collect the money. Sunday papers are the heaviest but they must be at the homes early or else the people raise hell. You've got to collect all of the money or else you and mom will get thrown out. The landlord's not a good man. I can't explain it, but you've got to get all of the money and get it home to mom. Some people won't want to pay; you tell them that they must because you and mom have got to pay rent. You're the man now. I'll ask tio to send money as soon as I get to Texas. I love you, Chulo. Stay close to Loveless. He's the best thing that's happened to this family in a long time."

Chulo's eyes clouded as he said, "I can take care of Mom." Ernesto left on the bus to Texas that afternoon.

The next morning at 4:00 A.M. Chulo was dressed and outside when the truck dropped off the bundle of newspapers. Chulo looked at the bundle as high as his waist. He cut the straps of nylon that held the papers and began to fold them in half and put them into the canvas bag. It was still dark when he finished folding the papers. He crawled under the canvas bag and tried to lift it. He could not even get it off the ground.

"Come in and eat something before you go, Chulo," his mother said. He went in and quickly ate his warm flour tortillas with beans and cheese; it was satisfying.

"Chulo, I know that you can deliver the papers by yourself, but I will help. Ernesto told me they must not be late. Today we shall not go to church, but I believe God will forgive us."

They walked outside, and his mother knelt down beside the canvas bag. "Chulo, help me put the straps over my shoulder." She crawled under the straps and at last the bag was in place.

"Stand, and I will help lift," said Chulo. His mother slowly stood, she seemed to be all right. A few steps later, she stepped on a rock and her ankle went sideways. She dropped to one knee. For a moment she was still.

Then Chulo heard her say, "I am alright. I was just clumsy. Help your foolish mother to stand again." Slowly she stood.

"Your knee is bleeding." She had a deep cut visible through her worn pants. Already there was much blood.

"It is nothing. Now let's go." As the sun came up they delivered the papers. His mother slowly walked and in time the load grew lighter. They were done in two hours. By then her ankle was quite swollen, but she did not complain.

When they arrived home the landlord was sitting on their porch. He wore new Levis and a clean white shirt. Chulo could not help but admire his cowboy hat and shiny belt buckle. Then Chulo noticed the way the man looked at his mother and hated him.

"Good morning. Your knee, it is hurt, and why the limp?"

"It is nothing."

"You have my rent?"

"I will have it later today."

"You know baby, this could be so much easier, so very easy. I have been good to you. Why can't you be good to me?"

Chulo's mother spit on the ground, her cheeks burning red, her strong hands on her hips, "Don't speak to me that way. You are filth. I will have your rent this afternoon."

"Me, filth? Listen, you will have my money by five o'clock this afternoon or you and your wetback sons will be on the streets. Don't play with me, woman." He grabbed her arm and looked into her eyes, "It could be very easy, so very easy." Chulo's mother pulled free.

The landlord grabbed her again, this time with both arms and tried to kiss her. Chulo grabbed at the landlord's legs, but the landlord flicked him aside.

Then Chulo heard Loveless. "It's way past time for you to be on your way."

The landlord stepped back and laughed, "What do we have here, the homeless lobsterman? I only let you leave your coffin here because it's an extra bit of cash. But listen, jailbird, I'll throw you out on your ass. Now run along."

Loveless stepped up onto the porch. In a flash the landlord had a knife out, and he was no longer smiling. He said, "You're on my property. If I kill you, it's my right. Now step the fuck off the porch and clear your shit off this property."

Loveless smiled and said, "I hope you know how to use that thing." Then the next thing Chulo knew, Loveless was clasping the landlord's wrist holding the knife, and with his other hand he was squeezing the landlord's balls. He must have been squeezing something fierce because the knife fell to the ground. The landlord was punching on Loveless with no effect. Loveless released his balls and snap-twisted the Landlord's arm so it was straight. Then, Loveless put his knee through the landlord's arm, breaking it like a thin branch. It was over.

Loveless grabbed the whimpering Landlord by the hair, lifting him slightly off the ground. The Landlord's arm hung awkwardly down his side, his breathing harsh and strained. Chulo was reminded of a time he saw a dog playing with a rat before he killed it.

Loveless asked him, "What kind of man behaves so badly in front of a child? What kind of man pushes a child to the ground and tries to kiss his mother? If you ever, and

I mean ever, get near these people again I will make you suffer, and then I will kill you *slowly*." Then he kneed the Landlord in the gut. Grabbing the back of the landlord's belt and hair, he threw him off the porch. The landlord landed in a cloud of dust and crawled to his truck. He spun his tires as he left.

Chulo's mother looked at Loveless with heated brown eyes and said, "You didn't need to do that."

"Yes, I did."

"Now you'll have to leave here."

"Not without you and your family. Will you go with me?"

"Yes." She hesitated, then said, "We have to finish up here though."

"We're finished here. Let's pack your things and load up my truck." Loveless scooped up a laughing Chulo and told him, "Go get your stuff together." Then he grabbed Chulo's mom and kissed her long and hard.

When they broke from their first kiss, Chulo's mother asked Loveless, "What took you so long?"

He replied, "Slow but sure, slow but sure."

To Struggle
With other
Creatures is the
Mind's worst disease.

Currents
Originally published in *The Surfer's Journal*

I remember that this girl had the nicest blue eyes I had ever seen. I was six years old. We were on vacation in Mazatlan and we were on the beach. I never found out the girl's name, never even talked to her. Yet, I almost died for her. I heard her say she was afraid of the waves. I had just mastered swimming that very summer and wanted to show her I was not afraid.

I started swimming out into the surf. When I was over my head, I looked back to see if she was watching. Something was not right. I was being swept down the beach so fast I could hardly see my fading family. I started doing the "Australian Crawl" just like my swimming teacher had taught me. The current carried me farther out to sea and down the coast. I was afraid and I was growing tired.

Then, seemingly out of nowhere, my father was by my side. I thought he was going to grab me and carry me to safety. He did not touch me. He just looked at me. Without saying a word, he swam towards shore. I was having trouble keeping my head out of the water. Every time a wave came, I struggled for air. I could tell that my father, who was not a strong swimmer, was tiring too. I wanted him to tell me it was going to be okay. He did not say a word. He just looked at me and continued his way towards shore.

Finally, I felt the beautiful sand beneath me. I crawled out of the ocean and vomited. My father, meanwhile, had gone back to where my family was waiting. Slowly, shamefully, I walked back to them, my head hanging low. When I looked up, I saw that the blue-eyed girl was looking at me. At least I had gotten her attention.

I was tired, scared, and confused as I approached my family. I walked up to my mother and father to apologize to them. My father slapped me so hard that I fell to the sand.

He pointed his finger at me and screamed, "Respect the ocean!" The girl with the beautiful blue eyes looked out to sea. To this day, I do not know whether to love or to hate him for that slap. *Now that I am a parent, I finally understand, that he was just afraid.*

Religion is a way of walking,
not a way of talking.

God

The minister was the holiest of men. He would not let you forget this. The small island was blessed by his visit. All of his entourage said so. He warned the islanders about the dangers of lust and greed. The minister told them that even thoughts of lust (oh yes, even thoughts) made them no better than dogs. He was the holiest of men. His gold watch, gold necklace and rings sparkled in the South Pacific sunlight. His styled hair held fast, even against the strong trade winds.

Zen 45

His wish was to see the island and to meet as many people as he could. He wished to save as many souls as he might from Satan, who lurked everywhere (yes, even in this room). Times were dangerous and people were disappearing because of Satan's followers. Nobody actually knew anyone who had disappeared but since the minister had said it, it certainly must be true.

The minister, along with his large support staff, toured the island and they were given nice meals and gifts wherever they went. The minister had heard stories of the hermit surfer who lived in a cave on the far side of the island. The surfer led a simple life. He fished using the ancient techniques and rode a long wooden board. Though the people tried to talk him out of it, the minister felt that he must bring this surfer into his fold.

The minister asked a fisherman in his flock to motor him to the far side of the island in his Skip Jack 28. They arrived at the bay where the hermit surfer lived in his cave. The minister rowed himself to the cave in the dinghy of the fishing boat. When the minister told the surfer that he was a man of God, the surfer welcomed him, for the surfer loved God with all his being and wished to live alone so that he could spend his days in quiet prayer and meditation. The minister asked how the surfer prayed. The surfer answered that he surfed waves cleanly and got as deep in the pit as he could. The minister grew quite concerned and told the hermit he must read the Bible or forever burn in Hell.

The surfer was frightened and quickly agreed to begin reading at once. The minister personally signed a shiny new bible and left it with him. The minister felt wonderful, for certainly he had saved another soul. Oh, how he loved to sign and give away shiny new Bibles.

The minister was tired, so he lay down for a nap while the surfer pored over the Bible. Shortly, the minister awoke and smiled as he saw the surfer reading with rapt intent. The minister bid the surfer farewell and rowed himself back to the waiting fisherman. They loaded up the dinghy and began their trip back to the other side of the island. After they had motored at 20 knots for about a half an hour they heard a voice behind them, coming from the sea. Swimming as fast as a dolphin, the surfer was catching up with the fishing boat. They stopped the boat, cut the engine, and the surfer swam alongside. He then churned up the ocean with his paddling feet until it seemed he was walking on the water itself.

The surfer said, "I have questions about the dreams and visions of Amos. Can you help me understand?"

The minister answered, "Come into the boat and let's talk." The surfer came over the rail. The minister continued speaking, "There are endless mysteries in the Bible. You could spend one thousand lives trying to understand it. I think you already know a peace I'll never know. Go. Just read it and know it's not to be completely understood by mortals."

"Thanks." The surfer replied. "Now I'd like to do something for you. Please remove your rings and put them on the seat." The minister did as he was asked. Then the surfer leaned towards him and removed his necklace and gently took off the minister's watch. He picked up the rings and held all the jewelry up in his right hand.

He smiled and said, "This is illusion," and threw the jewelry into the sea. The minister's eyes opened wide, then he started laughing from deep inside his chest. The surfer laughed too. Then he dove over the side and started swimming back to his cave.

Amongst the glitter,
Remember
You are of the ocean.

A Promise Broken

Once, not so long ago, there were two young men who were the best of friends. If you fought one of them, you fought both of them. They were named Micah and Kele. If one of them was hungry, both of them were hungry. Their home was on the west side of Maui. During their days they would ride their surfboards, play tennis, meet girls (as young men sometimes do), and read books. In the evenings they would go to their waiter jobs for the easy money. After work they would hit Spats at the Hyatt or Banana Moon at the Marriott. These were the euphoric, smoky days of youth. As time went on, they decided to try their luck in the clothing business.

It was not easy. They had no experience, just the seemingly endless energy of youth. The friends worked with blinders on for many months. Every cent of their money went into the business. From the beginning, the business was an equal partnership. They promised never to let the business come between their fine friendship. No amount of money could ever be equal to the friendship they shared.

Kele kept his night job because the money was needed. Micah spent all of his time and energy working on the business. Orders for their clothing began to come in, and the young men realized that their dream of financial independence was coming true.

They ventured to Long Beach, California, to show their clothing in the International Action Sports Retailer Show. The clothing was a success; they were on their way. They had so many orders that they could not afford to meet them. With the help of Los Angeles lawyers, they incorporated, and raised well over $500,000.00. Micah and Kele's friendship grew along with the business. It was an exciting time. Micah and Kele traveled all over America, Europe, and Japan to sell their clothing. The trips were always successful and it seemed as though they were blessed with good fortune. It didn't seem like work, it seemed like one endless, wild party.

Soon they leased offices in San Juan Capistrano. They opened their own stores and had a warehouse full of goods. They were at the top of their game and the good times were rolling. Then something changed.

Micah decided that he would hire his family. Kele adamantly disagreed, but Micah was determined. After weeks of turmoil and arguments, Micah's wife took over all the major accounts. Kele told Micah that this wasn't fair to the reps, but Micah said, "Family first."

Then Micah wanted to bring in his stepfather as the head of National Sales.

Kele said, "He's got absolutely no experience in fashion or sales."

Micah replied, "Family first."

Clearly, the business had ceased to be a partnership. The friendship, too, had ceased.What had once been a beautiful and strong brotherhood was now over. Kele was disappointed at what success had done to his once great friend. With a heavy heart and sad eyes, Kele resigned from the company.

Micah then hired his mother.

Less than a year later, the company was bankrupt. Kele returned to college to pursue other avenues. He was quite content, but I'm told he still missed the friendship he and Micah once shared.

Imagine Kele's surprise when, fifteen years later, Micah called him up to say he was sorry for not treating him like a friend those many years ago. It was a call that meant a lot to Kele.

*To quietly take
in the
elements
is to remove
the dust from
your soul*

Talks with Trees

I had never seen magic mushrooms before. I was living in Mammoth and we had guests all the time. A friend of a friend gave me a few caps and said that would be enough. I have always considered myself a bit of a wild man, so after he left our house I helped myself to a handful. I couldn't stand the taste of them so I swallowed them, like pills. One after another after another.

Zen 53

That morning I was supposed to meet my new girlfriend's brothers. I pulled up to her nice two-story house in my 1970 VW bus. She had some scam going where she embezzled around $5,000 a week from her job. I didn't know it at the time; I just thought she was rich. She was a little older than I, and she seemed worldly.

The throttle cable of my bus was snapped so I drove with the back hatch open and used a long wire to accelerate. I was disappointed that the mushrooms were having no effect. We sat down to breakfast. Her brothers seemed like pretty nice guys. Suddenly, I couldn't even look at the eggs; they were melting and sliding off the plate.

The cat outside the window became a giant mouse. I told everyone that I was coming on to shrooms for the first time, and they asked me if I had anymore. I told them I didn't. I went to my girlfriend's room to lie down. She came in to say goodbye. She was wearing Ray Bans with yellow lenses. I told her she looked ridiculous and started laughing hysterically. She got pissed off and left to go make some turns.

I thought if I relaxed for a while that I'd be okay. The room was swaying and moving all around me. There were colored towels that looked like psychedelic waterfalls. Explosions of color seemed to come out of nowhere. The wood grained walls started closing in on me. I had to get out of there.

I somehow got my bus up to the warming hut. I remember a parking attendant telling me to find a place to park. Luckily, I knew him. He looked at me and said, "Dude, you are out there." I parked the bus and stared at the ceiling. The little dots in the headliner became Van Gogh's Starry Night. I pulled myself from the car and made it to my locker.

I guess I started to freak because my friend E.J.

Zen 54

came in and asked me what the hell was going on. I told him I had eaten too many mushrooms and that I was scared. He laughed and said, "Don't fight it, go with it. Go make some turns, go fast, get big air!"

I dressed, grabbed my board, and headed to chair eight. Once on the lift I felt pretty good. There was light snow falling and the sun was playing hide-and-seek games. I studied the snowflakes on my glove and felt sure that each contained a universe. The snowflakes fell in blends of brilliant colors. Morphing and gliding into shapes and drops, like livid, undulating, dancers, moving in harmony, throwing their bodies across time and space.

At the top of the chair I saw my good friend Carlitos. He was sitting under a tree looking pretty lost. I could tell he'd been crying.

I boarded over to him and sat my bottom down next to him.

"What's up?" I said.

"Steak and Eggs just told me. Sonar's gone. He killed himself. Hung himself behind his house."

"What? Where's Canoe?" Canoe was Sonar's German Shepherd and best friend.

"Canoe's gone, that's why he killed himself. He went to Bishop and left Canoe in the back of his truck, like he always does, right? He went into the Auto Part store and when he came out Canoe was gone. He went fucking nuts looking for him. Last night he was outside the Rafters looking at the sky yelling and crying, 'You sit, good dog. You stay right there. I'm coming. You're a good dog. You're the best dog in the world. Good dog. Good stay. I'm coming for you. Canoe, Canoe.' I took him inside and asked him what the fuck he was talking about. He said he Knew Canoe must be dead, waiting for him in heaven, because there's no way anyone got him out of his truck-bed alive. Then, he said he wanted to go home so I walked with him out to his truck. He said he was okay and that everything was going to be all right. We smoked a fatty then he split. They found him hanging behind his house."

I sobered up pretty quickly. At least I thought I did. I asked Carlitos if he was okay. He said he was. I told him I needed to get higher into the mountains and asked him if he wanted to join me. He said no. I told him I'd check in with him in a day or two.

I headed to chair nine to find some fresh stuff on Dragon's Tail. The storm was a Nevada low, so the powder was uncommonly light. Time was doing funny things. I felt as if I had only made a few runs, boarding as hard as I had ever boarded before. Yet the clock at chair nine showed 3:00. I thought I would like to hike down the Tail on my last run. I hiked for a long time. Sometimes I stopped in order to cry.

Out loud I said, "Fucking Sonar. You son of a bitch. How could you do this to me? I love you, Sonar. I love you, Canoe."

I was pretty sure I knew where I could find some big air with a nice steep landing. I kept thinking it was just over the next ridge. I was out of it. The snow started coming hard. It was getting dark. I was one lost motherfucker.

I didn't give a shit. Sonar. I looked around. I had never slept in the snow before. I thought I was just like Jeremiah Johnson. I went to the biggest tree I could find and started digging under the thick overhang of limbs. I dug out a nice little snow cave at the base of the tree. I built up three walls facing the tree and made a roof of branches. By the time I finished it was dark and dumping snow. The tree enjoyed my company. I had proper clothes and, being a smoker, I had not one lighter but two.

I had some papers of various sorts in my wallet and

I used them to carefully start a small fire in my snow cave. A fire would be nice but not essential. I knew that if I needed to I could stay awake the whole night and walk out in the morning. As it turned out, I was able to make and maintain a sweet little fire.

I fed the flame and talked with the tree.

"Tree, Sonar was kind of smelly. Yeah. He didn't bathe too regular. You know? Huh? Do you? Once some really drunk frat guys started some shit at our party and Sonar jumped right in. He was skinny and wore thick black glasses, but he jumped in and hit some college kid across the head with a ski. Opened him right up. They left that party in a hurry and didn't come back. You should have seen how proud Sonar was. He was glowing that night. He even got laid by some chubby basket check girl. Fucking Sonar. And Canoe. You'll never see a dog as good as Canoe. The dog was smarter than Sonar. Tough son of a bitch too. You never saw Sonar without Canoe. They were a team. Sonar said that Canoe had been with him for many lives, ever since men lived with dogs. I guess that's why he thought he'd go after him."

I thought I would run out of tears, but I didn't until the first light of morning showed itself. The storm had let up some. Off far in the distance I saw a ski lift. I walked towards it.

If you love the sacred and despise the ordinary, you are still bobbing in the ocean of delusion.

-Lin Chi

Woman

Their hut rested just inside the dense jungle. The air was rich with fragrant mangos and flowers.

She held Rani close to her and whispered, "Do you know how much I love thee, my son, my heart, my Rani?" And Rani, who was five summers old, nuzzled his black hair into his mother's breasts and laughed, a laugh that touched his mother's insides in a way that only your own child can. When she looked at Rani she saw her husband, too. Her man. "We are a family," she thought, "This is my son, this is my hut. We have food and a canoe and a wave-riding board."

Her man had gone to ride the waves on the other side of the island. It was an all-day excursion. Whenever he returned from riding waves he would be his happiest. He said the ocean scrubbed away his grouchiness. Within her there grew a warmth that frightened her, for her life was so very good. Yes, when things were too good, she would sometimes be afraid; a woman's premonition.

Then Rani said, "Look at the pretty snakes, Mom." The woman climbed up on the high bed, holding Rani very close. The small, black, deadly mambas were half coiled in the doorway of the hut. The snakes were very young, and she knew there might be a nest of many nearby.

"Will they hurt us, Mommy? You said the black snakes were bad."

"Yes, the black ones are bad. But I am with you and those silly snakes can't get up here. You take a little nap, and I'll watch those black worms." She rocked Rani and watched the snakes. Rani wanted to study the snakes too. Finally, as the morning turned to afternoon, Rani fell asleep. Hours went by and the snakes watched them. The snakes seemed content to just sit there, mocking her. Then she began to frighten herself in ways that only a mother can. Her instinct to protect him was causing her to imagine what a mamba's bite would do to her son, her world, her life. Her thoughts drifted, "What if I have a heart attack right now? Who will guard my son?" God, how she wished her man was here. But he would not be back until nightfall. "If he were here," she thought, "he would laugh and smash the heads of the snakes."

She looked at his spear. Perhaps she could reach it. But could she reach it without setting down Rani? No. Surely she knew that Rani would roll in his sleep, right off the bed. Without putting Rani down, she stretched her slender brown arm and, just barely, reached the spear.

She imagined how her man would kill the snakes. He would use the spear to smash the snake's head. She set Rani down in the middle of the bed, never taking her eyes off the snakes. "Dear Lord, I'm scared," she thought. But she was more afraid of harm coming to her son. Then, to give her strength, she imagined the snake biting her son. Over and over she pictured this. It made her stronger. From within her rose a woman who was sure, protecting, and unafraid.

In her mind she spoke with the snakes. "So, you want my son then? Come on take him. There is only me between us. Come on."

Softly, she slid down from the bed. She held the

spear in front of her, her mind imagining that she had already been bitten. "You have bitten me; I'm not afraid then. You cannot kill me, devil. I am already dead. Sweet Jesus, let my spear fall sure."

She slowly lifted the spear and brought it down on the closest snake, sure, and almost true. But even in a half coil the snake was indeed a snake. The black mamba shot towards her lifting itself completely off the ground. But alas the warrior in the woman was quite awake, for she sidestepped the darting mamba and again brought her spear down swiftly and slammed the snake. For a moment it was stunned. And during that moment the woman called upon God himself to guide her spear. Her next blow nearly took off the snake's head and it was quite dead. Then she moved towards the other snake as it slithered out the door. She slapped down on it as it headed into the flora. It slowed and she beat on it over and over. Its purple and red insides were coming out from its ruptured reptile skin, and still she beat on it.

She was snapped out of her trance when she heard the laughter of Rani.

He poked his head out the door and said, "Mommy, you killed it enough." And his laughter filled the island, making it lighter, until the woman thought the island itself might float away, right into heaven.

From the withered tree,
A flower blooms.

The Eyes of Night
Originally published in *Surfing magazine*

He stood poised at the edge of the cliff above the *Bay*. The moon was full and he was alone with his thoughts. Yes, a bit of thinking before the step.

"Yeah, this way will be the best, a moment of fear, then splat. High tide will move in and clean up. End the voices of discontent; end the thoughts of utter darkness. Madness, oh madness, you tireless bitch. You won't leave me, you live in me, festering my being. Anyone who looks me in the eye knows that I'm no longer there, so no one will ever look into my emptiness again. No more dark thoughts, turn it off. TURN IT OFF!"

The young, blonde-haired, blue-eyed, 1980 surf star put his arms out as if he had wings. The island wind smelled of flowers. Waves swept in across the *Bay*. The moonlight lit up the night. The reflection looked like the sea floated a billion tiny fires. And for just a moment he knew silent peace.

But then he heard the softest cry. He was not sure if it was real, so he did not jump. He listened with his whole body. There it was again. Yes, he was sure now. He stepped back from the cliff and went towards the sound. Behind a tree he found a small piece of fur that contained the smallest breath of life. It was a kitten. It was filthy, and its eyes were scabbed over with blood and dried mucus.

He picked up the kitten and began to cry. The young man cried for all the world. He held the kitten and cradled it back and forth. The kitten responded by whimpering and purring. With a corner of his t-shirt he wiped the eyes of the kitten clean. In the moonlight, bright blue eyes stared back at him.

He took the kitten home and decided he needed to stick around and take care of it. The young man then focused on other goals. He told himself he'd go back to school and finish college. The kitten grew up to be healthy and strong. So did the man.

Try as much as possible to be wholly alive, with all your might, and when you laugh, laugh like hell and when you get angry, get good and angry. Try to be alive. You will be dead soon enough.

-William Saraoyan

Ain't Nobody's Business

When I was twelve years old and in ninth grade, we moved from the west side of Oahu to Imperial Beach, California. When we arrived in I.B., it was beyond my comprehension how we could have left paradise for such a cold, gray place. The truth was my father wanted to make some real money and he found opportunities in Hawaii limited. He was in the real estate game. Also, my oldest brother, Bull, went to military school in Long Beach. My folks just could not control him. He was (and is) one of my heroes.

I was shocked at how frigid the brown water was. I had scavenged a child-size beaver tail dive suit. Me and my beat-up Dewey Weber found our way to the ocean at every opportunity. After we had been in I.B. for a few weeks, three older boys started giving me a hard time. Maybe they were fifteen or sixteen. They didn't go to Mar Vista High; they must have been dropouts. They called me "Jungle Boy" or "Coconut Boy" with such hatred that I stung something fierce.

Before long they moved up to throwing rocks at me whenever they saw me. I figured if I stood up to them once they would leave me alone. Early one Saturday morning I headed out at Descanso St. Right when I got to the sand, rocks started coming from the boys. They were sitting around a fire. There were empty beer bottles around them and it was clear they had been there all night. A rock hit me in the face, and I went ahead and charged them. I got in a few good licks, and I slammed one guy with my knee between his legs. Then they beat me silly.

Growing up on the west side of Oahu I had been beaten up plenty of times, but this was different. They didn't stop. It was the first time I had my nose broken. Something was very wrong.

They started pounding my head into some rocks, one of them shouting, "Kill the nigger!" Finally, an old Asian fisherman started banging on them with his fishing pole. They started to go after him, but he used his fishing pole like a staff and whacked them pretty damn good. It warmed my heart. They scattered, and I ran all the way home, leaving my shitty old Dewey Weber behind. I wouldn't see that board again.

My father wasn't home a lot. He was a man that was driven to succeed. I don't know what lit the fire under him, but he was one of the most ambitious men I've ever known. My mother pretty much handled everything at home. This particular weekend he was out of town looking at some investment property in Los Angeles. My mother kind of lost it when she saw how beat up I was. She put some ice on my face and cleaned up my cuts with peroxide. Two of my teeth were chipped. She told me I could cry if I wanted, but I didn't. Coming from Hawaii, we always believed that we could handle our own problems, without the interference of police. I knew where one of the boys lived so my mother went over to have a word with his mother. I'll never forget how his mother yelled at mine.

She screamed, "Get off my property, you nigger-lipped bitch."

My mother smiled at her (and, boy, could she smile) and replied, "Well, I see where your boy learned his manners; the fruit never falls too far from the tree. Remember, I tried to talk this out." Then my mom stopped smiling and gave the woman a look I had never seen before. I saw that even my mom could forget she was a Christian sometimes. Because she spit on the ground and hissed at her, "You're an uneducated piece of fecal matter - look it up." Then she stared at her, daring her to come out of her house. The woman slammed her door. We walked home with our heads held high.

When we got home my mother got on the phone and called Bull's military academy. While she was waiting for my brother on the phone, she looked over at me and sang part of her favorite Billie Holiday song.

"If I should take a notion to jump into the ocean, ain't nobody's business if I do." Hearing her sing took my pain away. Bull had been in military school for two years and he was pretty much reformed. His problem had been his tendency to fight. He would fight anybody at any time. I remember when he was in junior high school he hopped over the counter at a liquor store and tried to fight a grown man. The man had been rude to my father. My father went over the counter to retrieve Bull, and a three-way brawl took place. I reckon my childhood was not your average one, but it's the only one I had. My mom got Bull on the phone and told him to pack his bags; he was coming home.

When my brother got home he didn't waste any time. His philosophy was that when you fight someone, you should mark up their face so they would never forget. He went over to their houses. If they weren't home, he told their parents to tell them Bull came by and that he had something for them. One by one he caught up with my tormentors. He was smaller than all of them, but they had hurt his little brother. He cleaned house with them. It was good to have him home. After making the streets and beaches safe for me, he never got into another fight. He went on to college, then graduated at the top of his law class. He now runs a very successful law firm in L.A. To this day I feel safer just knowing he's not far away.

Artists should be regular and ordinary in their lives, so they can be violent and original in their work.

-Flaubert

The Jet Ski Incident

Keone is only at home among the waves. He can function quite well on land; it's just that there is an unexplainable pull towards the sea. He wonders perhaps if in a past life he was a dolphin. He is a peaceful man. Keone is a loving husband and father, one who enjoys classical music and art. He strives to be a man of love.

But buried deep within the calm Keone lives an ancient warrior. A warrior who would rather not fight. A warrior who will go to great lengths to avoid conflict. A warrior who will only go into battle to kill.

Keone sat outside the pack. He always sat outside. Nobody ever took off on him more than once. It was something that just was not done. The surf was triple-overhead out of the northwest. The regular crew was out trading waves and hoots. Keone was compelled to take off as deep as possible and ride the life-giving swells until their energy was spent. As he rode the ocean's power, he thanked God for the day. He smiled as he thought of his wife and children. All was in balance.

It started as an irritating vibration in his inner ear. Then, from out of the north came the flying blue Jet Ski. Its rider was a muscular man. He wore a spring suit and his exposed skin was heavily tattooed. His head was shaved clean, and he wore a bushy, blond goatee. Keone's experience told him this man had done more than his share of time in the *government hotel*. The Jet Ski rider rode fast and sure. He darted in and around the ten or so surfers, laughing and spinning his ski in one place. Keone had never seen one ride a ski so well. The surfers yelled at the Jet Skier to get out. They all called him names and splashed water towards him. All the while Keone sat well outside and tried to release the Jet Skier from his mind. The noise, the smell, the wake of the Jet Ski. It began to eat at Keone. He tried to will away the rage that began to build in him. Then the Jet Skier buzzed out Keone's way.

Keone looked at the rider and roared, "YOU'RE PISSING IN MY CHURCH. THIS IS MY CHURCH AND YOU'RE MAKING IT DIRTY!"

The Jet Skier yelled back, "Fuck you bitch, I can ride here just like you."

Keone pointed his big yellow 10'2" gun towards the skier and shouted over the noise of the engine, "You're breaking the law. You need to be 200 yards outside of the breaking waves." Keone tried to get the C.F. numbers off the ski, but it had none.

The Jet Skier yelled back, "I make my own fucking laws." Then he buzzed close to Keone and whipped his ski covering Keone with spray.

"That's it!" yelled Keone and he charged the skier.

At first it was like a bullfight and Keone was the bull. He'd chase the skier and the skier would turn and taunt Keone.

Keone screamed, "If I catch you, I have to stop you."

Then it was the Jet Skier's turn to roar, "Come on then, Geronimo!"

And he charged straight at Keone full-speed.

Keone jumped to the nose of his board and swung the tail out in front of him. Then he brought his big single-fin out of the water and sunk the nose. Using the buoyancy of the board as a counter weight, he hurled it at the on-coming Jet Skier's head. Keone dove deep as his board landed on the head and shoulders of the Jet Skier, the fin slashing the Jet Skier's scalp. The Jet Skier had not fallen. He put his hand on his scalp and looked at his own blood. Then he came back at Keone screaming his war cry.

Keone had reappeared next to his board and resumed his position of battle. Fin out of the water in front of him. Then Keone noticed that he was no longer alone. The other surfers had joined him, ready to finish off the Jet Skier. The Jet Skier whipped around his ski and high-tailed it out, flipping off the surfers as he sped away.

Keone got a lot of waves that day. The Jet Skier hasn't been seen, smelled, or heard since.

*The greatest sin is
to be unconscious.
-Carl Jung*

Going Home

An earlier version of this story was originally published in
The Surfer's Journal

Prison. Inside. The institution. Jimmy knew he would not be going back. There are two kinds that get out. Some just get out to see how long they can make the party last. Jimmy was of the variety that wasn't going back, back to hell.

He was driving home from northern to southern California. He thought he'd hit the pier for a few before dark. A chunky, head-high southwest was coming through. Jimmy always gave respect to surfers no matter where he was. Dark hair, dark eyes. He was old school. No such thing as localism. He grew up in a world where one judged another surfer by his surfing. No bullshit. NO trash talking.

The set came and Jimmy let the hometown crew get the first few waves. It was their home break and Jimmy knew how important it was that a man get his waves. Then Jimmy was in the spot, and he glided across the choppy swell. The air smelled salty and the ride was satisfying. A blond kid tried to drop in on him as the wave began to reform, but Jimmy shot his board up and blocked the guy out. The guy started cackling at Jimmy.

He shouted, "Duh, duh, duh, look at him just fucking stand there, duh, duh, duh…"

Jimmy finished his ride, enjoying the power of the wave and riding it until his fin almost hit the sand. It had been seven very long years since he had ridden a wave. As he knee paddled back out, inside of him an anger began to build. He did not understand how this punk could talk to him like that. What was it that made the blond kid believe he could show such disrespect? The kid had a big TEAM laminate on his board. He looked to be about twenty years old.

Jimmy paddled up to him and quietly asked, "Why are you heckling me, kid?"

"You were just standing there like a fag, man." Then the yellow-haired punk waved his arms into the air and said, "Look at me, I'm a fag longboarder. Duh!"

Jimmy said very softly. "You don't know nothing about me, kid. You're so far out of line that you don't even know it." Just then a goateed guy who was about twenty-eight or so paddled up to Jimmy. Jimmy looked at the goateed man and knew he was soft. Yeah, he had lots of tats but they weren't done in prison. Neat and clean. Jimmy thought he could handle the goateed pretty boy without breaking a sweat.

The Goatee screamed, "What's the fucking problem? You hassling my friend?"

Jimmy stayed calm and replied, "Your skinny little boyfriend here has a big mouth. He's got to learn to keep it shut, not that it's any of your fucking business, *pretty boy*."

The Goatee said loud enough for all to hear, "Take it to the beach, you fucking kook. You're not the pier. Man, you are NOT the fucking pier!"

God, how Jimmy wished he were man enough to paddle away from him. He closed his eyes for half a moment and tried to will away the rage, but when he opened them there was the Goatee.

Jimmy looked at the Goatee and said loud enough for only him to hear, "I'm going to really enjoy hurting you." Jimmy felt alive.

Something changed in the Goatee when he saw the sharpness in Jimmy's eyes. The Goatee had expected Jimmy to back down like some schoolboy. Jimmy was no schoolboy.

"Ha!" yelled the Goatee and he quickly turned his board and sprinted for shore. He looked back at Jimmy and sort of stammered out, "You're going to fa-fa-fa-fight the whole fucking be-be-beach, you dumbshit!"

Jimmy breathed deeply. "So be it," he thought, "it's a fine evening." Jimmy slowed down his heart. He pictured the fin of his surfboard going into the Goatee's head. He visualized a handful of sand going into the eyes of the biggest guy whoever that might be. Yes, the biggest must go down and not get up. He thought about low, hard kicks, gouges, elbows, bites, and head butts. He also thought, "I don't fucking need this anymore." Then he snapped to and began a mantra over and over, "Keep them away. No groundwork. Keep them away."

Jimmy waited for a wave to come. The other surfers gave him space. He gracefully rode a wave in and as he approached the shore he grabbed a handful of sand. By keeping the sand in the hand that held his board, it was not noticeable. There were four guys waiting for Jimmy as he walked out of the water. Others seemed to be coming his way. For Jimmy, time seemed almost to stop. The biggest guy was easy to spot.

Jimmy knew him. He did not know him personally, but he knew his kind. The biggest one had tats from the inside. The largest tat surprised Jimmy. It said, *"Through Christ – End Racism."* His large round head was shaved so that it reflected the dying light of day. The Shaved Man had spent years in the institution lifting. His arms and chest were huge, but in the prison yard tradition his legs were skinny. Jimmy didn't look at anybody but him. The Goatee stood off behind him.

Jimmy looked at the shaved man and said "What happens when you go surf outside of the pier? I came in peace, but pretty boy here wants to take a crack at me. Give me just FIVE SECONDS with pretty boy, then we'll all dance." Jimmy knew the Shaved Man wasn't at all scared. But Jimmy picked up on a sense of fairness that sat behind the eyes of the Shaved Man.

The Shaved Man giggled like a crazy bastard and said, "Why not?"

The Goatee spit out, "That's bullshit! What's that? Five seconds? Fuck, lets just smash the kook." But the chemistry had changed. All eyes were on the Goatee. No one was going after Jimmy before the Goatee.

The Shaved Man looked at the Goatee and spoke evenly, "Seems like you don't jump into shit till it's about through. Go ahead, step on up, little man." It was clear that the Goatee wasn't interested in Jimmy one on one, not even for five seconds.

He started backing up and said as loudly as he could, "I'm over it!" Then he walked away and Jimmy knew that the Goatee was all through at the pier.

But then Jimmy saw the Goatee had found some sort of courage deep down in his sac and was charging him.

"I'm proud of you, pretty boy," Jimmy said as he threw his board and the sand in his hand aside. Pretty Boy came at Jimmy head down and swinging. Jimmy's first thought was, "This guy fights like a sixth grader." Then Jimmy jumped in the air and put his heel down hard on back of Pretty Boy's head. His neck snapped pretty good and he hit the sand with a thump. Before Pretty Boy could get up Jimmy stepped around him and kicked him in his ribs with four quick snaps. All the while Jimmy kept his eyes on the Shaved Man. The Shaved Man was laughing. Jimmy laughed too.

Pretty Boy started to slowly try and get up. He had

sand in his nose and mouth.

Jimmy said, "I wish you'd just stay down, I really don't want to have to finish this." Pretty Boy remained on his ass, holding his side.

The Shaved Man nodded towards the ocean and said to Jimmy, "You seem all right, brother. Why don't you go out and get some more?"

Jimmy answered, "No man. Thanks for the offer, but I won't surf here again. If you ever get to Sunset Cliffs, I owe you. I just want to go home."

The Shaved man nodded his head and said, "Go home then, brother, peace be with you."

We'll surf until we die.

-Windansea grommet

H.B. Surf Theater

Mystical things happened to me at H.B. Surf Theater. It seemed like every time I went there something out of the ordinary went down. Yeah, it was a given that our car would be broken into. The thing was, you had to hide your valuables where the thieves wouldn't find them. And the girls, they were older surfer girls that were completely out of our reach, making them all the more desirable. Yeah, mystical things happened to me at H.B. Surf Theater.

One Friday night I was heading out to see Five Summer Stories for the seventh time. My parents were out of town, and my sister's boyfriend was over. He was a surfer from Hermosa named Bob Cat, and he was completely out of control. I worshipped him. He insisted on making me one of his special smoothies before I left to go to the movie. He was laughing hysterically and the shake he made had a bitter taste. I drank it down just as my friends pulled into the driveway.

Boys will be boys. I had prescription glasses, and when I wore the "magic blazer" I could buy beer at Harbor Liquor. Yeah, there were bare asses thrown. Yeah, we were irresponsible and I know we were lucky to survive the insanity of it all. But we were young, surfers, and immortal.

While we waited in line for tickets my stomach began to feel queasy. I remembered how my sister's boyfriend laughed as I drank the "special smoothie." When I sat down in the theater, the screen seemed to be melting before my eyes. Colors dripped and ran down the screen as the movie began. The most brilliant fireworks display I had ever seen was going off all around me. When I closed my eyes it was even worse.

My seat began to free-fall beneath me. Down, down, down I went, spinning and dropping down the inside of a psychedelic tornado. I landed pretty hard on the sand of a deserted beach. The ocean was multicolored and alive, but the land was in black and white. My vision seemed grainy as I headed away from the ocean. I saw some buildings, so I headed towards them.

The buildings remained black and white but the people were unlike anything I had ever seen before. Fantastic colorful mohawks, bodies pierced in all the wrong places and people carrying machetes. It was twisted. I went into a bar called George's, and there were people lying all over the floor, twisting around on the tile with their eyes closed; I recognized that they were *mind surfing*. All along the bar there were Chinese water pipes set up. The bartender approached me and wanted to know what I'd like.

"What do you have?" I asked.

He brought out a tray of what looked like herbs. They were neatly separated and organized.

He answered, "I got some real nice Jose Angel here, smell it." He put the flowery green under my nose, and I knew it was good.

He continued, "I've got some Greg Noll that's heavy, or some Gerry Lopez that is really smooth. Of course, you can get funky with some Corky Carroll. It's all good. Personally, I go with the Duke, you know, Island fragrance. You're not from around here are you?"

"First time here."

"Really? All right, bra, I'm gonna give you something I've been saving for a special occasion." He pulled out a little wooden box and carefully opened it. He then put a small piece of the green into the bowl of a water pipe.

"Its Buttons, baby, take a rip."

I took one deep toke. Then another. I started coughing. Next thing I knew I was underwater holding my breath. I popped out from the warm sea and I was holding on to a bright yellow Local Motion stinger. I was at Kaisers. I felt different. I looked at the waves differently. I paddled into the lineup and took off deep behind the peak. As I entered the barrel I spun a 360, got pitted, spit out, did a layback, broke my fin out, got back in control, and flew out of the diminishing wave with a big smile. The other surfers were hooting something fierce! On the next wave I faded, made an insane rail-to-rail bottom turn, pulled under the curtain, got spit out from 15 yards deep, did a cutback reverse 360, picked up some speed and got air out the backdoor of the wave. On the next wave I took off way late, ate shit, got stuffed into one of the metal ribs that's under the water at Kaisers, panicked, and woke up in my seat at the H.B. Surf Theater. The theater was empty; the show had ended some time ago. I didn't know where my friends were. Mystical things happened to me at H.B. Surf Theater.

To go
to absorb
to smell awakened memories
are there Santa Anas?
is there a southern hemi?
I have arranged my life
around surf reports

To go there
to wait
to consider
but where did Red go?
where will I go?
I have measured my winters
by boat rides to Todos Santos

To go now
to struggle
limbs aching
why must I come here?
why must I leave?
I have measured my life
by solo journeys

In the end
it is an illusion
only our families matter

Aldo's Bus

Some VW buses are more special than others. The first time Chucky saw Aldo's bus, it made him ache for one. It was a 1970, blue on the bottom and white on top. The curtains were made out of Mexican blankets. It was one cool ride.

Somehow surfing brings friends together in a way that is solid. My closest friends are the friends I have surfed with all my life. Perhaps it's the fact that we know we may have to count on one another for our lives. Being air breathing creatures, the ocean is not our natural element. Every time a surfer enters the water he is automatically entered into the food chain, and if for some reason he is unable to keep his head above water, the outcome isn't pleasant.

Chucky got up early to catch the Fullerton beach bus on Saturday morning; he hated being an inlander, but as a fourteen year old it was out of his hands. He made his way to the beach bus, which left Fullerton Park every Saturday at 9:00 a.m. and returned at 5:00 p.m. When Chucky started to get on the bus with his surfboard, the new driver said no. Chucky pleaded, telling the new driver that he had brought his board on numerous times before. The driver didn't even look at him, he just said no. Chucky left the park quickly so no one would see that he was close to tears. He wanted to go surfing so badly, he couldn't stand it. The KMET surf report had said it was pumping.

My parents weren't the type to let me go on unsupervised surf trips when I was fourteen. So I did what some kids do; I lied to my folks. I told them I was going with the Mule's parents. I even carried my gear to the Mule's house. That's where Aldo picked us up. Aldo knew every trick when it came to camping. San Onofre campground was always full in the summer, but that didn't stop us from camping there. Aldo would pull up his magic bus right to the campground entrance and tell the ranger his friends were expecting him. He'd give the ranger some random name, and when the ranger couldn't find it, Aldo would politely say, "It's a large group, perhaps they put it under another name. Could I please go in and look for their cars?"

Aldo's style would pay off and the ranger would reply, "Sure, just let me know where you end up."

Chucky's head hung low as he walked home defeated. Then, lo and behold, who should pull up next to Chucky but Aldo. Aldo was a senior and Chucky was a freshman. Seniors weren't supposed to notice freshmen, but there was Aldo, smiling at Chucky.

"Need a ride to the beach?" asked Aldo.

Chucky's mind raced. Technically there was no way he should go. His parents thought he was going on the city beach bus, under the supervision of adults. But, hey, Aldo's got a bus, and he's almost an adult. Chucky knew his parents would disapprove.

"Sure man, thanks!" Chucky replied.

"How you set on cash?" Aldo asked.

"Gotta fiver."

"Let's go."

"Thanks man."

Aldo had a nose for opportunity. He'd seek out older girls who were camping alone. Then he'd explain that the campground was full and he and his friends would greatly appreciate it if we could share their space. Naturally we would provide beer for their hospitality. Aldo's charm was fatal and the girls usually said yes. Then we'd head back to the ranger with our new friend's name.

There's an unwritten rule in surfing that an older surfer will take a younger surfer under his wing and show him the ropes. It's a law as old as surfing. Aldo had chosen Chucky as his protégé. Aldo liked that Chucky had an absolute devotion to surfing. Chucky listened to every word Aldo said, and placed it in his permanent file. The two headed to 18th Street Newport. Aldo explained that the large south swell would be hitting there nicely. Chucky just smiled and hoped that someone he knew would see him riding shotgun in Aldo's bus. Aldo lit up a joint and handed it to Chucky. Chucky liked the smell.

Aldo, the Mule, and I were tight. We looked after one another in and out of the water. If somebody called one of us out, they called all of us out. Friends are friends. While sitting around the campfire at San Onofre we sipped our Schlitz Malt Liquors, smoked Aldo's crooked joints and talked about the wonder of it all. We toasted to Buttons, Gerry Lopez, Rory Russell, and Buzzy Kerbox. We all made efforts to hook up with girls, but Aldo was the only one to get to crawl into a cutie's sleeping bag. We slept under the stars and thought about surfing and surfer girls. We crashed hard into sleep and when we woke up in the day's first light, the Mule was gone. Sleeping bag and all, the Mule was nowhere in sight. We started tripping.

Aldo pulled right up to the curb in the no parking area of 18th Street. He got out of the V.W. bus, stretching his back. The surf was going off. Some blond guy who looked about seventeen or so was standing there checking out the surf. The blond kid was skinny and had a crew cut. Chucky recognized him as one of Quiksilver's up and coming.

The Quik guy looked at Aldo and said, "Quack quack." To quack at someone was to infer that they were a duck and therefore a kook.

Aldo looked at the Quik guy and softly asked, "Are you quacking at me, sticker boy?"

We searched all over the campground. We looked over the cliff and up and down the trails. The worst part was that the surf was cranking. Aldo thought he found some blood on the ground outside a locked bathroom. I told him it looked like ketchup, but he was sure it was blood. We banged on the bathroom door for five minutes. Then Aldo got an axe out of his van and broke the sturdy door down. There was no one in there. We walked away kind of quick and searched for another hour before alerting the rangers. They offered to call his parents but I told them I would do it. I was sort of choked up while I called the Mule's house. I didn't know what I was going to say to his folks. I sort of felt responsible.

Chucky got out of the bus. He wasn't very big, but he figured he'd be honored to stand by Aldo's side. The Quik guy walked up to Aldo and said, "Go home, inlander." Aldo stepped back away from the guy and said, "Oh yeah, shredder, why aren't you out there?"

"Shut up and leave, now!"

"I don't want to square off with you, but you'd better back off," hissed Aldo, his face becoming red and a vein pulsating on his forehead.

The Quik guy stepped up to Aldo and Aldo rabbit punched him in the nose, quick as you please. The punch was clean and crisp. The Quik guy's ugly nose bled, and

Chucky thought that it was lovely, yes, quite lovely.

The Quik guy was spraying buckets of spit as he hissed, "Don't piss me off. Just leave. I'm crazy, I tell you. I'll kill you. Man, you don't know me. You don't even want to get me started, I'm fucking crazy - I should be locked up."

The phone rang forever when finally I heard a very familiar voice say hello.

I said, "Who's this?" The answer I received made me both happy and mad.

"It's the Mule."

I screamed into the phone, "What the hell are you doing home? We've been looking all morning for you, we thought you were dead!"

The Mule replied, "My folks came and got me last night, I woke you up and told you. Don't you even remember? You were so out of it you don't even remember!"

I said, "You never woke me up, you son of a bitch. I'm glad you're okay, now we can go surfing."

Then the Quik guy walked towards Aldo. Chucky was a little scared thinking that the Quik guy might go into some *Kung Fu* mode. Aldo stepped back as the Quik guy came towards him. Smack! Aldo cracked him with another beautiful punch to the side of the Quick guy's head, and down he went.

From the ground the Quik guy repeated his credo in a quivering voice. "You'd better get the hell out of here. I'm trying to save your life. God knows I'm trying. " Then he got back to his feet. His nose was bleeding and he held the side of his head. He walked towards Aldo. By this time it seemed the Quik guy was sort of crying.

He babbled out, "Don't make me fuck you up, man you don't know who I am – you don't! I don't want to kill again."

He was actually pretty fast. He came right in to Aldo and bear hugged him straight on. Aldo just head butted the shit out of the guy's nose, squishing it flat. The Quik guy hit the sand hard, bleeding like a faucet.

As Chucky and Aldo walked away they could hear the Quik guy choking out the words, "You don't want to get me started, you don't want what I got."

Aldo turned to Chucky and said, "This beach reeks, let's hit Trestles." And so they did, and Trestles was doing its thing.

An autumn evening;
It is no light thing,
To be born a man.
                    -Issa

The Glide

The phone rang. Ryan's stomach turned. Of course his father would have to be home to pick it up.

Ryan started to leave the room, but his father said, "Hold on, Ryan."

After he got off the phone, he barked at Ryan to go get his surfboard. "That's it, I'm fucked," thought Ryan. "That's the end. Why did that bastard Peters have to call my house about a lousy F in math? Christ, get a life! The worst thing is, I fucking hate math. It gets so confusing that all I want to do is go for a surf to clear my aching head. Living on the sand of South Mission doesn't make it any easier." He grabbed his board from his room, a room like those of many other freshman boys at Mission Bay High School: the walls covered from top to bottom – every available inch - with pictures of his surfing heroes, like, Occy, Kong, Slater, Curren, Cheyne and others.

His mom sauntered into the living room as Ryan brought forth his board. She said, in a gin and tonic voice, "Honey, you can't take his board away."

"We've been too damn soft on him. For God's sake, the kid is flunking freshman algebra! No, I should have done this long ago." He took the board from Ryan and yelled, "Enough is enough!" as he leaned Ryan's beloved ultra-light Rusty onto a chair. Before they realized what he was going to do, he broke the board in half by stepping through it. "When you get a B in Algebra, I'll buy you a new board. Damn it! I've been where you're at. You've got to be strong to survive in this world. I put myself through dental school, and I'm not going to let your surfing destroy your grades. Surfing is a curse!" He stormed out of the three-story house, slamming the door behind him.

Ryan's mother just looked at Ryan and said, "I'm sorry. There's nothing I can do when he gets this way. I know how much you loved that board, Ryan. I'm sorry."

Ryan said, "He's a monster. I don't even think he's my real dad. A real dad wouldn't be such an absent asshole. Fuck. What? Now all of sudden he gives a shit about me? Too little too late."

"You think I'm going to let you talk that way about your father? You've got another thing coming, mister. Go to your room and figure out your math."

"Yeah, I'll go to my room; you go watch your idiot box. You think you're fooling anybody, *gossip queen*?" He punched a hole through the drywall as he tromped off.

The next morning Ryan didn't come down to eat. When his father went to check on him, what he found startled him. Ryan was curled up in a ball, and all the color was gone from his handsome face. He was feverish and had dark circles under his eyes.

"What's the matter son?"

"I'm just really tired, Dad."

"Come on, son, you're all right."

"Yeah Dad, I'm all right. I'm just tired."

"Get some sleep, you'll feel better. You know I did

what I had to do."

Ryan didn't feel up to going back to school. Day after day went by, and Ryan did not get better. His parents became concerned. Ryan was their only child. They told themselves that everything they did in their lives was for their son. There was, however, a broad, dark, ominous valley that lay between them, its depth hard to determine.

Ryan's parents had always given him *everything* he wanted except the thing he needed most. That was time with his dad and mom. More importantly, he needed at least some sort of guidance. Ryan's folks had let him grow up feral; they had not given him a sense of right and wrong. He could go where he wanted and when he wanted from the time he was three, night or day. The fact that he survived childhood was proof that God's angels keep very busy. When Ryan would lie, they thought it was cute. Values were for the poor. Who needed values when you were rich? His mother spent her days yakking with anyone who would listen to her poisonous words. Ryan never really knew if people liked him for himself, or because his family was rich. Indeed, deep down he wasn't at all sure what being a friend really meant, no one had taught him.

Ryan went days without eating. A doctor, who was close to the family, came to see him. Ryan did not care for this man, who smelled like a cold hospital.

"He's okay," said the doctor. "Needs to eat and drink some. Seems more than a mite sad. If he's not up and around soon we'll bring him in and run some tests. But I don't think it's physical. I suggest some counseling."

Weeks went by. When Ryan's father saw how skinny his son was becoming, he asked Ryan if maybe he wouldn't like to go out and buy a new Rusty or two. An F in math suddenly became something very unimportant, but Ryan's fire had gone out.

Ryan just said, "No thanks, Dad. I know you broke

my board because you love me. You do, don't you? For once, I think you do." The corners of Ryan's lips turned up a bit. "I'm just so tired. I'm not sure what I really saw in surfing anyway. It seems like it's been forever since I was a surfer. That seems so long ago, like that was somebody else. I just want to sleep."

Ryan's father grew desperate. The failing health of their son united Ryan's parents, and they called his friends to come and visit him. But Ryan didn't want to see anyone. He pleaded with his parents to keep his friends away, and they obeyed. They were losing him. They wanted to take him to the hospital, but he adamantly refused, as he had refused counseling.

When told that Ryan had completely lost his spark, a neighbor suggested they give his friend Skip Frye a call. Their neighbor knew that Ryan thought the world of Skip. Maybe Ryan would listen to him. Ryan's parents didn't hesitate. His dad called the shop on Felspar Street. When Ryan's father explained why he wanted to talk to Skip, Skip's wife, Donna, put him on the phone. After Skip heard what was going on he simply said, "Where do you live? I'm on my way."

When Skip arrived he spoke in hushed tones to Ryan's parents. Skip then asked if he might talk to Ryan alone. They said yes. Ryan's mother went into his room. The room had the sickly sweet smell that precedes death. The curtains were closed. Though it was mid-day, the room held very little light.

Through her whispery tears, she said, "Ryan, wake up. There's someone here to see you."

"Please don't make me see anyone," mumbled Ryan as he opened his tired eyes.

"It's Skip Frye."

"Skip Frye?"

"Yes, he'd like to visit with you. He's taking time out of his busy day."

After a long silence, Ryan said, "Okay."

Skip walked into Ryan's bedroom.

He wore faded blue jeans dusted with surfboard foam. He had on an old brown flannel shirt and his face was red and peeling, his blond hair close to his head. He looked a little like a homeless person to Ryan. Ryan liked that.

"There's waves today," said Skip, his voice soft and happy like a child's.

"Why are you here, Skip?"

"Thought we'd just talk awhile."

"Oh."

"Heard your dad broke your board."

"What? He told you? He's an ass."

"Yeah. Dads are a separate race. We try to do the best we can but God knows we screw up. I always wish I could go back in time and do things differently myself, but that's not how it works. We just have to learn from our mistakes and move on."

"Seems kind of useless, Skip. The whole fucking thing. Seems like it's all just bullshit."

"There's some truth in your words. You know you and I share something. We share a father, Ryan."

"Come again. What do you mean?"

"God the father. The father of Jesus. He's our father too, you and I."

"Not the Jesus stuff. I really don't believe in that, Skip. You know, put your faith in things you can touch and all that." Ryan sat up a little in bed.

"You'll have to trust me on this one, Ryan. Christ is the real deal. God is our true father, and he teaches us to forgive. Can you forgive your father, Ryan?"

"I thought it was me who needed forgiving."

"Maybe in some ways it's both of you. Forgiveness can totally set you free. People who can't forgive are buried in their own sadness, like I think you might be."

"Who is Jesus? I mean, who is he really? No bullshit."

"Ryan, when he was dying on the cross, he knew that someday I would be telling you about him. Even as he suffered unimaginable pain, he thought of us, of this conversation."

"You think so? Come on Skip."

"I'm betting my life on it. In my heart I feel his love. It helps me have a little balance. Balance, Ryan. It takes a long time, but you gotta find balance."

They sat silently while the shadows moved across the room.

"Balance," whispered Ryan.

"Balance," repeated Skip.

"Balance, ying and yang, negative positive, heaven and hell," said Ryan a little more loudly as he sat up taller.

"See, Ryan, if you can surf all day, everyday, it loses its magic. I grew up watching guys just surf. They keep waiting for that perfect day that will never come. They don't realize that, with Christ, everyday is perfect, as long as you earn your surf."

"I don't surf anymore, Skip. That was someone else from one of those real old black-and-white movies. I just want to stay here in my room. It's safe here."

"What are you afraid of, Ryan?"

"I don't know. Skip, I wish I did. I'm just afraid." Ryan's eyes grew moist and minutes grinded by.

"It's all right to cry, Ryan. Let it out now. It's okay to be afraid. Man, this planet can be a frightening place. You just gotta find a place to glide. Ponce de Leon went

Zen 97

searching all over for the Fountain of Youth, but it was under his feet the whole time. In the end, he bothered the Indians so much they finally killed him." Skip's laughter filled the room. "The ocean is the fountain of youth. Have you ever seen the old guys in the Tourmaline parking lot in the morning?"

"Yeah, yeah, I've seen them listening to Hawaiian music and drinking coffee." Ryan's eyes were brighter now, listening to Skip's words, remembering the older men, their camper trucks and their grizzled laughter. The aged boys leaned their colorful boards against a wire fence.

"Those old geezers are just little kids in old men's clothing. They found their glide, Ryan. They found the balance. But it takes a long time to find that. Some people never find it throughout their whole lives. Some people never get to smell the rocks at low tide when the sun is just coming up over Sunset Cliffs. Some people never get to hear the seagulls laugh as they drop into a PB Point bomb. You remember your *first wave,* Ryan?"

"Yeah. Clearly. When I was six, we went on vacation to Waikiki. My dad let me rent a longboard."

"What was your first wave like, Ryan?"

"The board was an orange log. I went out pretty far and took off on some white water. I got to my knees, then I was standing. It's kind of weird because I remember looking up at the hotels and the mountains while I rode the wave. Then I fell and had to swim after the board."

"Then what happened?"

"The board went pretty far in. I remember being able to smell the coconut suntan oil coming from all the bodies on the beach. Then I got to the board and paddled it back out. I stayed out there all day long. Man, was I hungry when I got out. I had a plate lunch, then some shave ice. I ate and ate and ate."

Skip opened the green curtains. The day was sort of

cloudy, but you knew the sun was going to win. They didn't talk for awhile, an easy quiet. Finally Ryan spoke.

"You know what, Skip? I'm starving, plus, I've been getting bored out of my mind."

"What sounds good to eat?"

"A plate lunch. Then some ice cream."

"I know a place, best plate lunch in town. My treat. Before you get dressed, you'd better take a shower. You smell a little ripe. See you in the living room." Skip smiled and started walking out. Just before he went through the door he said, "Ryan, just give Jesus a little thought now and then. I'm just planting a seed."

"Okay Skip."

Four months later Ryan woke up to the sound of surf thundering. The *Santa Anas* were blowing straight offshore. He knew the jetty would be all-time. He looked at his new Rusty, then thought about an algebra test he had later that day. Ryan had a cute math tutor now and he suspected he was going to kick ass on that test. He touched the small silver necklace she had given him, then turned his back on the waves and went to school.

He whispered to himself, "I hope it's still good after school." There was a bounce in his step.

Letters from Maui

November 2, 1979

Dear Carlitos,

I read a quote on the plane flying over here. It made me think of you and your child-like zeal. It's by Pablo Picasso and it goes, *"It takes a long time to become young."*

I got here three days ago. I spent the first two nights in my rental-wreck, fighting off mosquitoes. I finally tracked down my friend, the Mule. He had a few days off from the Hyatt, and I didn't know where he was staying. All's well now, selling my bus to get over here was worth it.

Yesterday the Bay went off. I hung around Keiki Bowl for awhile then paddled out for a few. The crowd was thick and the pecking order was very well organized. This guy named Fruit Bean just charged. There's a really skinny kid named Porter who was surfing just like a puppet. His arms and legs are all gaggles, but he just wouldn't be knocked down. Bradshaw was out; he seemed pretty cool. He and Porter took off on a monster; Porter was behind Bradshaw. Anyway, I thought they were both gonna get crucified when they pulled into this macking, cavernous, blue hole. Bradshaw came flying out wearing a huge smile.

Zen 100

I had given up on Porter when he came shooting out from behind the spit. His shorts were wrapped around his ankles, and he was laughing like a madman. Word is, though, he's doing too much blow.

Biting clouds on the Rock,

Spidey

P.S. Can you please sell my sailboard and gear for a quick $250.00? Send it ASAP.

January 2, 1980

Dear Baby Brim,

Wow, brother, this is a whole other world. It's like there's a different sort of law over here. I lent my car to Jimmy the other night. He had a date with some hot tourist. He got drunk and totaled the front end on a light post. Nobody got hurt, but it sure turned my life upside-down.

I didn't have the money to change the registration right away. I planned on doing it but cash is tight. So the police towed the car away and billed and cited the girl who I bought the car from. Last night this local guy (not huge but plenty mad) came walking right into our apartment and just started raising hell.

He kept yelling, "My dad's the Chief of Police! I'll have you fucking guys killed! Fix this mess tomorrow or you're all dead, and don't try to leave the island cause you're being watched." Over and over he kept screaming the same thing. I was going to go ahead and try and take him out but chose to heed Sun Tzu and "not attack the enemy unless it is critical." Something about him seemed a little unbalanced. I always have to remind myself that the only enemy is fear.

Tell Mom the usual: I'm healthy and only hanging with nice girls (all I can!).

Zen 101

These are the smoky days,
Bro

March 15, 1980

Dear Carlitos,

Thanks for the cash. It's crazy. I work for forty hours life-guarding at the Marriott but I'm poor as shit. After we three pay the rent for our one bedroom at Honokowai Palms, I'm about broke. I make a few dollars a day in stupid towel-boy tips. The girls and women are sickening. It's just a silly smorgasbord of sin. There's waves, women, bud, and good friends. Why do I seem so unhappy then? Sometimes I feel like I'm Siddhartha when he lives an empty life of lust.

We spear what fish we can, but the water's not always clear in Honokowai. Sometimes for dinner it's rice and butter, then for dessert it's rice and syrup. While I'm at work I can eat during my breaks. I've got it down, and every available moment I'm in the employee dining room stuffing myself like a coyote. We also find food around the neighborhood: mangoes, bananas, and pineapples.

I was in Lahaina yesterday when this guy (who threatened to kill me - that car thing) started yelling at me. My friend Keone asked me if I was going to let that punk talk to me that way. I told him his dad was Chief of Police, and Keone started laughing like hell. He said, "That kook's been here about a year; he's from Colorado."

I chased that sucker down and marked up his face pretty good. He fought like a girl. I sort of lost my temper and was hammering him when Keone pulled me off. We left him on the sidewalk outside Kimo's. He was crying and saying, "I'm out of here, I'm out of here, I'm gone!"

Can you please see what you can get for my skis? Sell all three pair, try to get at least $150.00 each, but take whatever you can get. We're fucking starving most of the time. When are you coming over?

Cannablissfully yours,
Spidey

January 1981

Dear Sis,

Thanks for the money surprise; it made life seem okay again. God, I miss Tara. I think that in life we meet certain people who will radically change the course of our lives. They're like a rock in a river. They are going to change your course. Tara was that person for me. She was the first one who explained to me that there was no honor in stealing. She told me honor was the only thing we'd bring with us when we meet God; everything else was of little or no importance. She told me not to be jealous of other's successes, but to celebrate them.

Sis, did you know Dad used to teach me to steal? Yeah, I knew it was wrong but I was just a child. We would take extra things from people who would trust us. You know, we'd pay for three palm trees but take four. Stuff like that. I really don't know what Dad was thinking. When I stole, he was so proud of me, and that's something I still crave. I'm going to be a different parent.

Tara took me in under her wing in Mammoth and hooked me up with the rental shop and my ski pass. It was such a new thing for me to hang out with someone who believed in righteousness sooooo much.

The last night I saw her she grabbed me and said, "Give me a kiss, doll, I might not ever see you again. I'm going to Tahoe with these guys." I looked over and they looked nice enough. Tara was a grown-up girl who could make her own decisions. I went for a swim in her Pacific blue eyes and kissed her goodbye.

Late that night I woke up and KNEW something

Zen 103

terrible had happened. I couldn't figure out what was wrong. I was really scared. I went outside and sat under a tree. I sort of *drifted up* and out of my body and somehow I was sitting on the branch of the tree looking at myself. My body was healthy, just sitting there on the ground. But somehow I was up in the tree. I jumped back down into "myself" and went in to bed. The next day I found out we had lost Tara in a car accident. A seat belt would have saved her life. You and the kids WEAR YOUR SEATBELTS!

The thing I'll never get over is that her dad got me through the next few days. Her father got me through it! His love, his life, his baby girl, his universe, his joy was now with God and he got me through it. I heard he went to see the driver of the car. He was in Mono County jail for driving under the influence. There was a lot of coke involved. I heard he told the young man that he forgave him. He told him not to let it ruin his life. He said he understood that they were young and they partied. His forgiveness is beyond my imagination.

After the funeral I just sat alone in the empty church. Her dad came and sat next to me. He put his arm around me, and I cried harder than I've ever cried. The day had been stormy and cloudy, but at that moment the sun burst out and shone through the stained glass windows.

He whispered to me, "She's still with us. She'll always be with us. She loved you so much. No, let me say that differently. She loves you so much."

Christ, how I hurt for Tara's mother and father. I want them to know how she changed my life forever. I want them to know that she lives inside me every single moment. I want to tell them that I love them, but I just don't know how.

Love,
Your little brother

Do not seek to follow in the footsteps of the men of old; seek what they sought.

-Basho

The Necklace

An earlier version was originally published
in *SURFER Magazine*

And so it was that the two surfers rode upon the island waters. In ways that cannot be understood by the Philistines, the surfers rode with the abandonment of those who reside in the shadow of knowledge.

At last did these two approach the sand. One of them, whom the people called Ice, glowed with the health that comes from a table full of fresh food. The other, who the people called Tosh, was of the skinny variety and had red eyes that spoke of hunger.

And so it was that Ice said to Tosh, "Come and live in my home. Eat at my full table and know the peace of a full stomach and rich surroundings."

And to this Tosh replied, in his warm, child-like voice, "Why is it that you live in such a large house with fine food, endless music, many guests, and women in such abundance?"

"It is because of my sponsor. They provide me with these riches so that I may focus entirely on my surfing. They have seen you surf, and they wish for you to come in out of nature's harshness and enter the sanctuary of their company."

"And what is it that I must do for the company?"

"Nothing. Simply wear this necklace that bears their logo." For a moment Tosh stared at the shiny necklace.

Then he said, "I see that you are cared for. But even a golden cage confines."

And the surfers walked their own way. One into the welcoming forest, the other into his golden cage.

But the forest wind blew cold through the restless trees and there was no food to be gathered. Tosh thought about Ice's warm sanctuary, and he found himself at his door. Ice kept his word and welcomed Tosh into his golden home and gave him food from his bountiful table, and glowing clothing, which caused Tosh to know pride. Tosh put the shiny company necklace around his handsome neck.

And then it was Tosh who saw a blonde woman dancing in a warm pool of water, and she beckoned him forth to her and said to Tosh, "I am Cali, come and bathe with me." And so Tosh came to know her and her charms. He spent his long nights in her sweet fragrance and his days out surfing upon the water. Soon the once pure Tosh came to know the warmth of wine and the aroma of sweet tobacco and the pleasures of the dice. His lean body became softer and his sweet breath became bitter.

Zen 107

His wave riding did not release the pain of walking the earth, until it was that Tosh thought to swim into the calm night ocean. He took off his clothes and swam out until the island lights were barely visible.

He treaded water and looked upon the stars themselves and asked aloud, "Who is this rat of a man Tosh who knows the bile and foul taste of wine and loses himself completely in a woman and dice and all the tastes and smells and sweet tobaccos that cloud my mind, costing me my peace?"

He swam as deeply as he could, thinking that his time on earth was through. Ten feet deep and he could still see the moonlight. Twenty feet deep and he started to feel it in his ears. Thirty feet deep and the light grew dimmer as a long Tiger shark swam by him. He barked an underwater war cry and the shark swam away. Forty feet deep and his lungs began to heat up. Fifty feet deep and his hands began to go numb. Sixty feet deep and his arms were also numb. Then, he *did not* want to die. He slowly kicked up towards the moonlight. When he broke the surface it seemed as though his body had forgotten how to breathe, then it remembered, and the air was sweet. He coughed, then slowly swam back to the island.

A memory was awakened in him that spoke of a simpler time when he needed to find his own food and warmth and pleasures. His feet touched the soft sand, and he walked naked out of the sea.

And the smell of it, oh the freedom of being reborn into the life of the spinning earth itself, the fish, the kelp, the sand, the rocks, the bird's dung, the decaying dead, the mist of the dying waves, the lightness of all of it spoke to Tosh, and Tosh did listen.

Far into the sea did Tosh fling the necklace, and again he entered the welcoming forest, vowing never to desire the trappings of the world.

Zen 108

Amongst the turmoil, hang onto your craft.

Swept Away

The winter of 93-94 will forever be etched in my memory. I explained to my wife that I had never, in all my years of surfing, seen anything like it. The waves just kept coming day after day. Huge, clean outer-reef waves that were everything I needed, and more. My wife could not understand the physical need I had to be out there every day. I couldn't explain it. We fought.

At one point she told me, "Just surf on weekends, you don't need to surf during the week."

I told her, "You don't even know me."

She replied, "If you don't like it here, you can leave."

"I can't be a good husband or father and just surf weekends. All right then, I'll leave." At that point she understood just what it meant to me. We worked things out.

One gusty, early afternoon I pulled into the Windansea lot. It was a cold weekday, and the beach was almost deserted. The waves were closing out from Simmons, all the way across to Big Rock. It was maxing. The faces of the waves were at least a bumpy twenty feet; no one was surfing.

Since the birth of our daughter I try not to surf alone. Sometimes, though, there's just no else out. On this particular day I decided to see if I could make the paddle out. I'm not sure why, I just thought I'd give it a go. There was no one on the beach.

I suited up, put on my leg-rope, and grabbed my 10'2" Randy Rarick. I wasn't sure which of my two leg-ropes to use. One was really thick for big waves, but old and a bit worn. The other was newer but thinner. I went with the older, thicker one. I studied the ocean and saw a river-like current running out just north of Big Rock. Sometimes, when I surf in demanding conditions, I seem to go on autopilot. It's not that I can't control myself; it's just like I'm standing outside of my body and watching. I paddled for about forty-five minutes.

I kept telling myself, "Just see if you can make it."

I was hanging onto my board as much as possible and getting pushed around pretty hard. Finally, I saw a break in the waves and paddled frantically out. I made it. I felt pretty damn good.

When I looked towards shore, I saw that I was drifting radically south. My plan was to catch a wave, ride it as far as possible, then straighten out and come in. I hadn't figured on such a strong current. I paddled hard north for about thirty minutes and enjoyed being out in the large, moving water.

Zen 111

I decided it was time to catch a wave in. Fear is like a giant switch in me. Suddenly it's on. The waves seemed to be getting bigger. It's funny what your mind will do to you when you let it. I calmed myself down, spun my board around, and committed to a big, bumpy, closeout right. The wave was sucking out so much water in front of it that the drop seemed like a mountain slope. I finally angled to the bottom and made my turn. The wave let me harness her power for a good forty yards before she closed out on me.

I never saw the lip coming. I had straightened out and was trying to "get small" in front of the wave when I got hammered. I hadn't counted on being knocked off my board; usually I can straighten out and prone. You hear about people saying they're never afraid. Well, I was scared, and even under water I could feel the power of the next wave coming down on me. I was under for some time and realized it was a two-wave hold-down turning into a three-wave hold-down. I had curled up into a ball so as not to be injured by my board. I opened up my body and fought with everything I had for the surface. As I broke into the sweet sunlight, I felt the leg rope stretching. It snapped; it was a lonely feeling.

For me, everything changes in a rough sea without a board. I was too far inside to swim to the safety of the deep, but I was a half-mile from land. The ocean was taking me quickly south. I was in a hell of a rip current. In no time I was way past Big Rock, heading for Hogan's.

All I could think about was getting air. I would get a breath then have to swim under the oncoming whitewater. I wondered if anyone from shore had seen me or if my body would be found. I wondered if my little girl would know what kind of man I was and if my wife knew how much I loved her. She wouldn't know. She wouldn't know!

When I realized I needed to tell my wife how much I loved her, my strength renewed.

Zen 112

I thought, "God, she's everything to me. In a billion years I'll never meet anyone like her again. My Beanie, my good, good woman, the mother of my Stormy." I was in trouble, but at least I was fighting. I realized my only hope for my immediate survival was to get out of the treacherous rip and swim beyond the waves. The outside waves backed off enough to let me swim out.

Once out to sea I knew I had only one chance, and that chance was in staying calm. If I could get to Little Makaha there might be someone out there surfing. We could "buddy" up on a board and make it in. The current helped me along. My wetsuit was on the thick side and helped me float. I just kept thinking that I had to get to my wife and daughter.

When I got to Little Makaha there was no one out that I could see. Even from the back, the waves there looked frightening. I decided I had to try and get to shore in the Bird Rock area. "I love you, I love you, I love you." I said it over and over, picturing my blue-eyed wife and brown-eyed daughter.

I heard the sound of an engine, and over the choppy sea I saw a lobster boat. I screamed for all I was worth, waving my arms like crazy. I yelled with everything I had. I saw the boat stop; it seemed to turn towards me, then it headed away. I treaded water. The energy I had spent yelling and waving had taken a lot of my fire.

The rip current going south seemed to be losing some of its juice as it hit the deep water between Little Makaha and South Bird. I put my head down and started swimming. The current had let up considerably and I was able to get to where the waves were breaking. I thought about trying to body surf a wave towards shore, but I wasn't sure I could survive that. So I waited between sets then swam towards shore with my remaining strength. I let the surf do most of the work. I finally dragged myself out

Zen 113

of the water at PB point.

The tide wasn't too high, so I walked carefully on the slippery rocks into the cove. I slowly climbed to the top of the stairs, and when I got there I sat on the bench and closed my eyes for a long time.

*Amongst the stingrays,
let your presence
be known.*

The Broken Board

I saved every penny I had for six months to buy my first surfboard blank. I was in the seventh grade and that new blank was the most exciting thing that had ever happened to me. I had mowed lawns, washed cars, collected cans, and babysat brats for that piece of foam.

I loved that blank. I spent every free moment with it, cutting, filing, and sanding. I had a special place in the garage where I kept it - on a rack, out of the way - a place where no harm could come to it. It was ready to be glassed. I knew this guy off Main Street in Huntington who was going to glass it for thirty-five dollars. I finally had saved the money for the glass job, and I was fired up to get the board finished. It was a simple pintail.

Every afternoon around five, I would seek the shelter of my bedroom. It was around this time that my father would get home from his office. My father's mood was always completely unpredictable. When possible, I just stayed clear of him. He hit the bottle pretty hard. One afternoon I was in my room when I heard the electric garage door open. He was home.

He stormed into my room and yelled, "You son of a bitch! You left your goddamned board in the way. I got so mad, I accidentally closed the garage door on my Mercedes."

My mind raced. Had I left the board out of place? No way! I ran past him expecting a smack, which didn't come. I reached the garage and had my worst fears confirmed. He had broken my board in half. He had scratched his precious car and was so angry that he had to do something. So he broke my board.

That's the moment I knew I would soon have to stand up to him. I wasn't going to let him get away with this kind of crap when I got bigger.

Before long I did get bigger. Then one day, when we were going to have yet another fist fight, I looked at him and he was an old man. That's the day I left his house.

He's long since gone due to his drinking. Even today, when nature breaks one of my surfboards, it only makes me stronger. But make no mistake. I wouldn't have had any other father in the entire world. My dad not only gave me the gift of life, he gave me the gift of the sea. And for that I will be eternally grateful.

Whoever saves one life,

saves the world entire.

-The Talmud

My Old Man

I was cold. So cold. I couldn't feel my legs or feet. I could wiggle my toes, though, so I was surprisingly optimistic. I told the ambulance attendant that I was freezing, and he gently covered me with a heated blanket.

I said, "I want to remember all of this, every detail. I'm going to write about it." I started laughing hysterically. Then I remembered Big Sid, and I started crying pretty hard.

*　　　　　　　*　　　　　　　*

In October of 1996 conditions were right for Spidey's Reef. Minus tide and a very solid northwest swell. Spidey's Reef is fickle and heavy. Because of the volatile and small swell window, it isn't accessible by boat. You just can't anchor safely and still watch your boat while you surf. It can only be reached by a long, slippery walk, and an even longer, interesting paddle.

My number one surfing partner is Big Sid. It's never too heavy for Big Sid. We were in the water just after sunrise, surfing alone. The wave at Spidey's is a relatively short right-hander. It breaks top to bottom for about fifty yards right in front of an exposed tabletop reef. As long as you stay away from the reef it's an insane, square wave.

We had traded waves for about an hour before I got dry-reefed. I was high and tight when my outside rail caught, and somehow I straightened out in front of the lip. I was unable to pull back into the tube because I became "locked in track." I would probably have been all right if I just would have jumped off my board. But the wave did something to me that no wave had ever done before. The falling lip landed behind me and bounced up over me. I was riding a completely white, beautiful moving bubble. It was surreal. Then all hell broke loose.

The next thing I remember was being turned about in a very unhealthy way. I was pinned to the reef, and my back was somehow getting pretty twisted. Then it felt like a giant took a sharp axe and split the bottom of my spine with all his might. I couldn't move my legs, and I had to fight not to pass out. The good thing was that the wave pushed me pretty high and dry on the reef. My leg rope had snapped and I couldn't see my board, not that I cared.

Fear is a son of a bitch. I couldn't see Big Sid. I pretty much panicked. I was trying to drag myself farther up the reef, but my own childhood voice kept whispering in my mind, "Am I going to die? Am I going to die?" I saw a set approaching, and I continued to drag myself higher up on the reef. I was slipping in and out of consciousness, my vision dimming. It was so odd to look at my legs and not be able to move or feel them. They seemed so tremendously heavy, like dead pieces of meat. The pain was so blinding that my mind wanted to let go. I knew if I let myself go unconscious, I'd probably be dragged back out to sea and would drown. I was screaming for Big Sid, but I couldn't see him. It seemed like I had been hurt for such a long time, but in retrospect I realize that very little real time had passed.

The white water from a wave exploded onto the tabletop reef and tried to pull me back into the sea. I hung

Zen 120

on tight, and felt like I was fighting demons. The grasping, dark spirits tried to rip me off the rocks and take me home. And still my own internal voice whispered, "Am I going to die?"

Then I remembered visiting deep, rural Mexico with my family when I was five years old. I drank some bad water and was in a terrible way. I mean, I hadn't kept down food or water for about five days. I remembered asking my father if I was going to die. He cried warm tears and told me he wouldn't let me die. I liked feeling his love so much that I asked him over and over, "Am I going to die?"

Each time I asked him, he cried even harder and cradled me in his tattooed arms, saying, "I won't let you die, Keone. I won't let you die." The spirit of my father was with me then on the reef, telling me he wouldn't let me die. I pulled myself higher out of the ocean's grasp and held on through the long set.

Then Big Sid was there. He had been thrown over the falls and landed on his fin, which had penetrated his stomach and his insides were hanging out. He pressed them in with one bloody hand and grabbed me with his other. He dragged me off the rocks, but my back hurt so much that I passed out.

When I awoke, there was a paramedic strapping me to a board to support my back. I asked him about Big Sid.

He said, "Your friend is one tough fucker. He hiked out and flagged down a car. He's pretty fucked up. The danger's going to be the infection that's sure to follow. His wound was dirty, plus he's lost a lot of blood. That's some friend you have there."

"Yeah. Big Sid. Hey, do you see our boards?"

Six months later Big Sid and I surfed Spidey's Reef again. It was pretty good.

Zen 121

To paddle quietly

is the

eternal now.

A Kept Promise

One morning long ago, while I was driving to San Diego State, 91X let San Diego know that the surf was thundering. The ocean is my church: the stronger the swell, the more enlightening the sermon. Like any other religious zealot, I did a U-turn and headed home to get my equipment.

After I chose a board and grabbed my wetsuit, I headed for Sunset Cliffs. I was new to San Diego and had heard that the Cliffs were the place when it was big. As soon as I pulled up I knew I was "undergunned." In other words, I should have brought a longer, gunnier board. The waves were triple to quadruple overhead, and I would have been much more comfortable on a nine-foot gun. The board I had with me was six feet, six inches. I put on my wetsuit and prepared to paddle out.

Until that day, I had taken the surf of California lightly. After surfing the Islands for six seasons, I felt fairly strong and confident in most California conditions. There were only two other surfers out, and I could not believe my good fortune. Giant, throwing, glassy walls and no crowd. The tide was very high; to get in the water I would have to jump about fifteen feet off a cliff. I studied the ocean for a few minutes and saw a sandy beach about a quarter mile south. I planned to paddle to that beach after my session. I should have studied the situation longer, but the learning curve in life can sometimes be steep.

I paddled out during a lull in the sets. As I paddled into the "take-off" zone, a set loomed on the horizon. Only then did I realize how truly big the waves were. My heart was pounding and I loved it. After riding two dream-like waves I began to feel strong and fluid. On my third wave I took off deep, behind the peak, and turned hard off the bottom of the steep blue wall. I shot back up to the top of the cresting wave and lost control as I brought the board around. I was launched into the air and free fell into the dark pit of the wave.

The wave picked me up and threw me over the falls. I felt small, confused. Which way was up? I was doing somersaults under the water, covering my head to protect it from my board or the rocky bottom. I told myself to relax, to save my oxygen. My lungs burned. The pressure in my head as I tumbled was painful. I opened my eyes and saw light amongst the turmoil. I was having trouble getting to the surface so I climbed my leash like a rope and finally got my head out of the water. I jumped on my board and thanked Jesus that my leash had not snapped. I began to paddle south; I was beaten and had had enough for the day.

In my mind I sang a little tune from a childhood cartoon, "Frizzle frazzle, frazzle frome, time for this one to come home." I heard a boom towards land and looked. To my unbelieving eyes, there loomed terra firma. I could not believe that I had been driven all the way in. The noise of the waves hitting the cliffs was deafening. The cliff looked like jagged towers of unforgiving rock. As the ocean exploded on the cliff, the white water shot skyward with a force that would certainly crush me.

I continued to fight southward, trying to get around the oncoming water. I was now within twenty feet of the cliff, duck-diving wave after wave. My arms were already heavy from being held under so long, and my mind was getting cloudy. I conversed with myself, "Don't panic, stay calm, breathe. Inhale through your nose, exhale through your mouth." I was now within ten feet of the cliffs. I noticed the barnacles, and I was jealous of their safe situation. Thoughts shouted out in my mind, "THEY'LL REMEMBER YOU. Relax. They'll remember you. It'll be quick. Relax." I was now within five feet of the cliff, and I could smell the animal life that fiercely clung to it. "TO HELL WITH RELAXING! I'm not gonna die, gonna fight." I scratched and clawed my way south, the cliff now so close that twice I pushed off of it with my feet. I could hear another set approaching; the waves looked like moving mountains.

Then I felt her. She was inside me, around me. She was the water and the mist. I felt my grandmother surround me. From inside my head she told me to come towards her. North of me, in the churning water, I saw her clear eyes. To go north was to go inside the belly of the beast. The water in that direction was solid white, an avalanche in full motion. I felt strong again. The next set was almost upon me. I pointed my board north and stroked for my life.

The current carried me faster than I could paddle. It was all I could do to hold on to my speeding board. I was moving so quickly north that the cliffs became a blur. Faster and faster, farther and farther, until I was deposited into relatively calm water. It happened very quickly, too quickly to be of this world. I paddled way out and around the surf, south, to the sandy beach. I walked out of the water and sat on the sand to think.

My grandmother had been confined to a wheelchair for as long as I had known her. Our parents had told us that losing her oldest son was too much for her. Subsequently, she was nearly consumed by arthritis. Though physically disabled, she had not been spiritually quieted.

She and my grandfather had migrated from Mexico City in 1923 and spoke very little English. They didn't have much money but worked hard. Grandfather picked fruit, and grandmother worked at Hunt's canning factory. Before long they bought their first house. Then they bought another and another. When my grandparents passed away they owned ten houses. They never learned English.

Because my parents wanted us to be "good Americans" we were not taught Spanish (a pity, but another story). Despite the fact that my grandmother and I did not share a language, we got on quite well. We communicated without speech. She could speak to me from inside my head, and I could speak to her too. Because I was a child, I didn't know this was unusual, I just figured some people communicated this way.

Five years ago, just before she died, she looked at me and I understood. With her clear, kind, bright brown-eyes she made her feelings known; she would never leave me. Her body might cease to be, but she and I would always be connected. She taught me that people didn't die, but journeyed ahead to be with Jesus. She had promised never to leave me. She kept that promise.

Aloha Todd Chesser
Originally published in *SURFER magazine*

We are all connected
we are all alone
we know the possible price
yet out there we are home

I pray for his family
I pray for his friends
that God will grant some strength
for Todd's memory will never end

but after the tears have washed away
though for some they never will
one must smile for just a moment
and know Todd's with us still

The Richest Man

Hard times. Keone had lived with them for a good part of his life. To him they weren't hard times, just life. On his morning run he looks for mangos that the night wind may have blown down. He keeps tabs on the small bananas that grow all around his Honokowai, Maui, neighborhood. When the water's clear, he spears a fish or two. Then the rent goes up. No warning, just another $200.00 a month. "Not right now," thinks Keone.

Then his neighbor Sol says she'll rent him her walk-in closet. You know Sol. She's the girl that was invisible in high school. Brown eyes, brown hair. Then, after high school, she just blossomed. Keone thinks she's the most beautiful girl on the island, too beautiful for someone like him, way out of his league.

The rent is cheap and the timing is right, so Keone says okay. He moves in, all his possessions fitting in a duffle bag. Sol has a little boy who's four years old. The boy's father is some musician who blew through town and won't be coming back. Sol is a good woman. Fit, hard working. She teaches aerobics at the Hyatt. Her workouts are so demanding that her nickname is "The Punisher." Her little boy's name is Bali. He's a tow-head with big brown eyes, and cute as a koala bear, but he suffers from asthma. Keone moves into the walk-in closet, which turns out to be hot as hell. No windows, no moving air. Little Bali has trouble breathing when he sleeps. He keeps Keone up most of the night with his hacking, congested, cough. Sol tries to comfort Bali so that he might get the rest that little boys need. Bali is Sol's whole life; she doesn't mind that his nose is always dripping mucus. Finally Keone gets up out of his closet and tries to comfort Bali. By holding him in his strong arms and gently swaying him, Keone gets him to sleep. Bali has gotten mucus all over Keone, and he is surprised it doesn't really bother him. When he hands the sleeping Bali to Sol, he sees tears in her eyes. He thinks, "God, she's beautiful."

In the morning Keone gets up and rides his beat up ten-speed to his poolside attendant job at the Marriott. As he works he scans the pool area for lost change or jewelry. He usually finds at least two dollars a day in change and he's not above picking up pennies. Keone has a secret, though. He only pretends to be poor. Over the course of his seven years of employment with the Marriott, he has squirreled away over $43,000.00 in the Bank of Hawaii. When he first started saving, he made a vow to himself that he wouldn't spend a penny until he reached $40,000.00, but he kept right on saving. Taking care of the large pool is one of Keone's responsibilities. Everyday he puts on a mask and snorkel and inspects the pool for cracks. At least once a week he finds jewelry on the bottom of the pool. He has found too many diamonds and other precious stones to remember. He's found anklets, bracelets, necklaces, earrings, and many, many rings. He has a connection in Lahaina with a jeweler. The jeweler gives Keone top dollar for all he finds then uses the found jewelry to create his own unique designs. The jeweler is quite talented and successful. Keone doesn't feel at all guilty about his "found jewelry" enterprise. He's saved seven people from drowning, and he gets paid eight dollars an hour. Six of the rescues were in the ocean. One was in the pool. He figures it all balances out. Girls and women let him know that they have time for him. He's been a pool boy a good long while and the thrill of tourist girls has long since waned. At night he goes home to Sol and Bali, and it's starting to feel comfortable. This concerns Keone because attachment is not something he wants. Better to be free to come and go, surf when he wants to, sleep when he wants to.

It's getting difficult to get much rest because Bali wants to be held by Keone most of the night. Bali's asthma seems to be getting worse. The heat in the apartment is incredible. The complex is called the "Sunrise" but everyone calls it the "Slumrise." The noise around the apartment is nonstop: music, yelling, fights, cars, and slamming doors.

The Tongans next door shoot heroin and deal in it, too. At night, the biggest Tongan shadow boxes for hours on end in the parking lot. They do not bother Sol, Kimo, or Keone though because they are local. Yet Keone is having trouble living in the walk-in closet, the walls are beginning to close in on him. And, he's worried that Bali is starting to get too close for comfort. Keone has always been alone, and that's how he likes it. At least that's what he tells himself.

The next day at work the tennis pro at the Marriott offers him a room in her condo. She'll charge what he's paying now. The condo overlooks Honolua Bay, and there is maid service. The condo is owned by the tennis pro's wealthy father. There is a Jeep that Keone can use. The tennis pro is not first string; she's a show pony. High maintenance, pretty when dolled up. Behind her back she's called "Plastica" because of her boob job and dyed blonde hair.

Keone thinks about it for a few seconds, then says, "My lucky day. I'll take the room." The tennis pro's eyes show Keone his reflection. Her name's Ashley. When she says goodbye to Keone, she shakes his hand but doesn't want to let go. He pulls his hand away, thinking, "Her skin is cold."

He tells Sol he's taken another room. Sol looks away and doesn't say anything. Bali cries and gets mucus on his Elmo shirt.

As he's walking out the door, Bali runs after Keone, his face streaked with tears, "Come back, Keone, don't leave, please don't leave, come back!" Keone stops and turns around. He scoops up Bali and gives him a bear hug.

He tells him, "I'll come back and visit, little man. I'll come back, I'm not going far."

Bali squeezes Keone with all the might his four-year-old arms can muster and whispers, "You need to live with me, Daddy." Keone sets him down quickly and grabs his board and duffle bag containing his meager possessions. Then he hops into a black Jeep that he does not own. He starts the engine, and Sol walks up to the window.

She puts her head close to his and looks him between the eyes. She tells him, "Thank you. You always have a place with us. You make Bali happier than I've ever seen him. You make me happy, too." Then she kisses him quickly on the lips and walks away.

Keone is confused. He thinks, "I'll be damned if I will ever understand women." He puts the Jeep in gear and drives away. The wind in his hair feels good, and he pushes the accelerator down to the floorboard. He turns the radio up as loud as it will go; "My Sharona" rocks the Jeep. He arrives at the condo, which is in a gated community. The condo is large, and there is air conditioning. In his room there are fresh sunflowers and two rolled joints in an ashtray by the bed. The smell of the joints is very nice. In the kitchen the refrigerator is full of meat, cheese, beer, and sweets. Keone marvels at his good fortune. He grabs the joints and goes for a quick surf, enjoying the use of the Jeep and no longer having to ride his bike or hitchhike for a surf. There's a new swell, and the crowds are light. Keone feels like he should be really happy, but there's an emptiness creeping up on him like an illness.

Evening comes. Ashley has made him teriyaki chicken with cashews, asparagus with hollandaise sauce, and wild rice, all served with an excellent Australian chardonnay. For dessert there's macadamia nut ice cream over fresh homemade brownies covered with hot fudge.

They sit down in front of the TV, and Ashley throws in a porn movie. She takes off her shirt and she's wearing nothing but her tennis skirt. She comes right up to him and sits on his lap, straddling him like a motorcycle.

She whispers, "I've been waiting a long time for this. I'm going to teach you things you've never dreamed of." Just then Keone thinks he hears Bali and Sol crying. He wonders how the wind carried their cries so far. Keone looks into the tennis pro's eyes and sees Sol. The sound of crying grows louder.

He asks Ashley, "Do you hear crying?"

"No. I'm going to be pouting if you don't get busy." Then she leans in, her red mouth open for a kiss, her breath stale.

But Keone is sure he hears crying. He knows it's impossible because Bali and Sol are over five miles away, but he hears their cries as if they are in the next room.

"I've got to go." He turns his head away from her kiss and stands up.

"You've got to go? What the fuck is that?" Her face turns ugly and shows her years. "You bastard." She tries to slap him, but he catches her hand. She's crying angry tears. She pulls away and puts her shirt back on.

"I'm leaving. Will you give me a ride?"

"Fuck you. Get out of here. Get out! Get out! Get out!" Keone grabs his board and duffle bag and leaves. He walks out of the gated community and there's a cab on the side of the road, waiting for a fare.

Zen132

Keone asks the old Asian driver if he can get a ride to Honokowai, and he says, "Sure." Keone rolls down one of the back windows and puts his board and duffle bag in the back seat. He hops in the front seat, and off they go. When they reach Honokowai, Keone pays the six-dollar fare with a twenty.

He tells the driver, "Keep the change, Uncle, it's payday."

Keone knocks on Sol and Bali's door. Bali opens it, shouts a bark of joy and jumps into Keone's arms. He's crying and laughing at the same time, saying "Daddy, Daddy, Daddy."

Keone holds him and says, "I'm home, little one. I'm home now. Shhhhhhh."

Then Sol is standing there. Her hair is down and she has a yellow orchid in her ear. She's wearing a white summer dress with tan sandals that wrap halfway up her muscled calf. Keone picks her up and carries both of them into the hot apartment.

Sol says, "Bali was crying for you. I guess I was too."

"I know. I heard you. That's why I came. Can I stay?"

"Will you?"

"I thought you'd never ask." Then he brushes a tear away from her content face, and they share a quick, warm kiss with their brown eyes open.

Keone says, "Start packing, we're out of this dump. There's something I need to share with you. With you and Bali."

*I write in vain,
for words
cannot tell
of the waves
of yesterday,
tomorrow,
and today.*

The Fire Dance

Originally published in *The Surfer's Journal*

Many generations ago, there lived a gathering of small brown children. They lived on a warm, sun-filled island. The children rode beautiful, long wooden boards, which they glided gracefully over the rushing blue waves. In the evenings, the children danced around the warm fire, singing their chants of joy and life. They danced each night without fail.

All of the islanders knew happiness, all but one. One boy named Kele had heard the ancient songs, which told of the Mainland far away. The songs told of wondrous wisdom and riches to be found on the Mainland. Kele longed to journey there and find these wonders, to discover the truth of the songs. Kele asked the other children if they would join him. They told him he was a fool and he would perish at sea. Kele did not listen; he knew he must go.

One evening he paddled with the west wind towards the Mainland. He worked through three days and nights. At times the sea was so rough that he thought he would surely die. At the end of the third day, he noticed a change, which gave him strength. His arms and face had grown hair. His body, once small and thin, had become large and muscular. With the setting sun, the Mainland came into view.

On the Mainland, Kele worked in a factory and learned how to earn small pieces of gold. He learned that people will steal from one another, given the chance. He did not understand what he saw. It was a place without aloha. After forty days and forty nights on the Mainland, Kele returned to the water's edge and found his old canoe.

It was a long paddle back. Kele's arms were sore and his face was beaten by the weather. A great storm tried to tear him away from his canoe, but his grip was strong. A warm east wind came up on his back and blew him to the island of brown children.

The children cried tears of joy when they saw that Kele had returned. He tried to tell the children about the Mainland, but they grew bored. They left him so that they might surf the evening glass. When night came, the children began to dance around the fire. Kele, too, began to dance. He danced around the fire in a frenzy, sweating and crying. Around and around the fire he went, through the night. Just before sunrise, his muscular body became leaner. With each circle, his manly face became more and more youthful. When the sun rose, Kele was a boy again. He vowed never to leave his island.

Amongst the confusion release your intuitive sight.

Gameshow Gets Married

Three weeks ago, my good friend Gameshow got married. This may seem of little importance, but Gameshow is an extremely free spirit. He does not settle down easily. We sat back in the preacher's chambers, waiting for the ceremony to begin. I could see he was as nervous as hell. I asked him when he had decided to marry Summer. He sat down, lit a cigarette, took a deep drink of his fourth vodka and orange juice, and started talking.

"Okay, this is what happened. Summer and I got into this huge friggin' fight about our relationship. After three years, she felt she deserved a commitment out of me. Can you imagine? She even threatened to leave me. So I told her, 'Go ahead and leave me baby, I ain't holding you back. Don't let the door hit your hiney.'

"I was kinda pissed, so I went surfing at Crystal Pier. It was Labor Day, so the blackball rule was in effect, you know, no surfing. There were no lifeguards in sight, and the waves were really good, so I paddled out. It wasn't long before a lifeguard in a Jeep pulled up and called me out of the water with his loudspeaker. I got out and, naturally, as soon as he was out of sight, I went right back surfing.

"The guards were back in force after I had caught about four sweet waves. I think they were jealous because I was ripping so hard. There were two Jeeps on the beach, and a red patrol boat came flying around the pier. Two of the guards were swimming from shore, and the boat was almost on top of me. I couldn't let them get me. I was in some trouble in the Islands, and there were some people looking for me. It was a money thing, you know? If these guards ran a check on me, I'd be taken in. Of course, Summer's Dad has cleared all that up.

"Anyway, I pretended to begin paddling towards shore. A set came, so the boat had to head out to sea. Then I made a break north, paddling towards PB point. I figured that if I could get to the cliffs, I'd be okay. I thought about what would happen to me if the guards caught me. I'd be put in jail. They'd put me in a cage. I was pumped up and paddling hard. I knew then that I couldn't let Summer leave me. I don't know why, all of a sudden I knew I'd be making the biggest mistake of my life if I let her go. I told God that if I got away, I'd ask her to marry me.

"There was a white-haired guard that swam like a wahoo. He swam faster than I could paddle; he was a freak of a swimmer. Before long, he grabbed my leash. I told him that I would go in; he had worked hard to catch me, and he wasn't going to let me go. As we walked out of the water, I began to think of Summer and what would happen. I looked towards the waves and said to the guard, 'Looks like that kid's in trouble.' His eyes darted towards the ocean and I swung the rail of my board into his gut with all my might. He doubled over, and I headed back out to sea. I was zigzagging towards the cliffs, and the Jeeps could no longer follow me. It was now just me, and the patrol boat.

"My energy level was screaming, pure adrenaline. The boat could not get close to me because of the swell. I saw the trail that I needed. I took a wave to the base of the trail and threw my board back out to sea. I wouldn't be able to run with it, and it was a piece of crap anyway. I scrambled to the top of the cliff and started huffing it. I ran inland two blocks to La Jolla Blvd., then headed towards PB. When I got home Summer was packing her clothes. I got on one knee and bit the bullet. I figured, what the hell, it's something new, right?"

"Right, like committing to a huge wave."

Pray to God, but hammer away.
-Spanish Proverb

The Outcasts 2034

I was off road in Cabo. I hunted waves alone. I know that before the Magnificent War people surfed together, but that was a long time ago, before I was even born. I pulled up on a small point and set up camp. I figured I'd stay until it was time to move on. Being one of a million or so citizens that inhabit North America makes one get used to being alone. I had my rig set up to run on corn alcohol, but I didn't drive more than I had to.

Just after dark someone called out, "Hello the camp." Christ, I was in the middle of nowhere, a spider in a web.

I responded, "Come on in nice and slow. Keep your hands where I can see'em." I grabbed my spear gun, which I always kept close and ready.

He came out of the darkness. The first thing I noticed was his baldhead and tremendous size of the man. His hands, his goddamned hands looked like they could break stones. He was maybe fifty years old, fifty hard years. His eyes were gray, cold, and empty.

He squatted Kiwi style and asked, "You got any grub?"

I watched him closely and motioned towards my pan of fried fish. I kept the spear gun in my hand, as always, cocked and ready.

He ate real slow, then started rambling in a whisper I could barely hear. He had lived before the Magnificent War. He looked at my boards and said, "I used to surf." The hoarseness of his voice was almost hypnotizing. I tried not to let my guard down. Deep inside me I knew he could kill me if he chose to. His vibration was intense and harsh, but I thought maybe he wasn't going to be trouble. I've never been a good judge of character.

He continued, his voice rising, "Nobody used to live outside the great walls. You see, the Machine provided for your every want. And Buddha, the surf! Oh, the Oceans were my blanket and the sky was my pillow and the long clean glide, that, like a woman shelters you from the omnipotence of maladroit politicians that are drunk with loquacious power that always escape to sleep, perchance to dream, of shelter from the arsenic-ridden sycophants that lead us through this rabble rouse. You see?" And then he looked right through me and continued with his stream-of-consciousness tale.

"There was a schedule. A fucking surf schedule. If you wanted to surf the morning glass you had to wait for your rotation. To do this thing and that thing, you see? They didn't know, they just didn't know. I was from the Lotus Sector. Goddamned best sector you ever did see, points and reefs. None of that bullshit beach break crap. Fuck beach breaks, fuck pretenders. Goddamn it, they had it all wrong. They taught little trolls in the child fabrication centers that 'SHORTBOARDS ARE GOOD, LONGBOARDS ARE BAD. ONLY WAVES THAT BREAK TOP TO BOTTOM ARE GOOD. THERE IS NO STYLE IN STANDING STILL.' The fucking pretenders couldn't even see, they couldn't see that they had been

Zen 143

taken. They missed more waves then they caught, they didn't make sections they should have. They were just wigglers masturbating on little disco boards. See, they thought I was a model citizen. They thought they had my balls, but I fooled them. They weren't so bloody smart. Yeah, they threw Virtual Reality crap at us every night. It was okay, if you scored some good cannabis bars. They started giving em out towards the end. 'A bar will take your smile far.' They fucking sedated us while the greedy oil mongers raped our world." Then he stood up real slow and lifted his hands as if he were praying. He looked at the new stars, and the firelight danced off his massive frame. His voice was loud and strong now and shook the earth itself. "BY ALL THE GODS, TOMORROW WILL BE A DAY OF RECKONING!" Then he laid down into the fetal position and continued, his voice once again a slow, hoarse whisper. "Achilles said that after Patroclus was slain outside the walls of Troy just before it was written that 'Who gathers knowledge gathers pain' which came just after the Ingush proverb, 'He who thinks of the consequences cannot be brave' which came before Machiavelli, 'Though fraud in all other actions be odious, yet in matters of war it is laudable and glorious and he who overcomes his enemies by stratagem, is as much to be praised as he who over comes them by force.' But then one morning I fucking woke up and could see. I don't know why, but I could see the strings on all the puppets. And then the Freemen must have seen it in my eyes, cause they came to me, you know? They snuck me letters, and I helped them get food and knives. After they knew they could trust me they told me about the outside. I made my break and went and lived outside the walls." His eyes moistened and he continued, smiling like a child. "Outside we lived how man should live. We hunted the ocean for our food. When the majestic surf came alive, all else ceased. We rode and

Zen 144

we laughed and we lived, and it was good. Then the machine fucked it all up and decided it was time for another holy war, as if war could actually be holy. Blew the whole egg to shit. Sadly, for the good of the Earth, it's better. Yeah, even degeneration is some sort of evolution. It was time for the walls to come down. See we're starting all over again. In another two thousand years we'll be right back where we left off. Thanks for the fish, kid."

The whispering man walked back into the night. Then, like an afterthought, he came at me. He had almost caught me dreaming. Almost. Right before he fell upon me I shot my spear right into his Adam's apple. It's my favorite shot, I call it a "gill" shot. He went down quickly, his hands trying to pull out the spear. I stepped back and watched him die. Then he stopped thrashing around and lay still. When I approached his dead body, he had a grin on his face.

I threw two big logs on my fire and went to find something I'd been saving for awhile. It was a bottle of special teriyaki marinade.

I am a part of all that I have met.
-Alfred, Lord Tennyson

The Voices of Baja Malibu

I am alive. I live and breathe. I was built by a man named Julian Paz. He and his friends built me in 1959. I live on a cliff. If there is one sadness in my life, it is that I am only lived in part-time. A house lives and breathes through its occupants. I am only truly content when my builders are safely within my strong walls where I can protect them. I like to hear their laughter and their children playing. I like to smell the foods cooking and hear my builder's music. I am not immortal. Like you, gentle reader, I was born, I am living, and I will crumble back into the earth. I can travel. I live inside everyone who has ever loved me.

Today I traveled with the grandson of Julian Paz. He went to La Puente, California, to give Julian's eulogy. There was not a better man in the grandson's life. Julian gave the boy the gift of exuberance.

Zen 147

The grandson spoke to the people in the church, "Earlier today I saw my nephew, Alan, and he looked so sad. So I asked him to walk with me. I wanted to tell him how happy we should be to have known his great grandfather. I wanted to tell him how we should hope to live such a life. But when I looked into his brown eyes I saw my grandfather in him. And at that moment I missed my grandfather so much I could hardly stand it.

"The last time I saw my grandfather was two weeks ago. I told him that the happiest times of my childhood were the times he and my grandmother took me fishing out of San Diego. He smiled and told me, 'We'll go fishing again.' And we will.

"When I was a boy my grandfather would hold out two hands. He'd say, 'Pick a hand.' Whichever hand I chose held a silver dollar. When I won the dollar, I felt both lucky and smart. For some reason I didn't realize until recently that both hands held a silver dollar. He taught me what it felt like to win, and I carry that with me today.

"When I was with my grandparents, they watched me the way only grandparents can watch a child. I remember sleeping in the back of their camper as we drove through the night heading for Seaforth Landing. I'd look at the sparkling lights of Mission Bay, and the world seemed clean and brand new. I felt safe, for they never took their eyes off of me. If I were hungry on the boat, they'd buy me a hamburger. If I were still hungry, they'd buy me another one.

"If you knew my grandfather, you would never go without. He fed the hungry. He loaned money to his neighbors. He taught me that when you give, you get back. His house was full of good food and Mariachi music. There was no garbage in my grandfather's house. In my grandfather's house YOU WOULD BE TREATED WITH RESPECT. In my grandfather's house YOU WOULD BE

JUDGED BY YOUR ACTIONS. He kept a loaded rifle behind his recliner, and I knew that, if need be, he'd use it. That's the kind of man he was.

"I had my own Ernest Hemingway for a grandfather. If you knew him, he will be with you for the rest of your life, for Julian Paz is a movable feast. I can't say I know for sure what my grandfather would say if he were here. But I think he'd say, 'Thanks for coming, be careful.'"

Within my solid walls I have kept a young woman warm against the elements. I listened to her anguish. I saw her write endless letters pleading with her lost love; a man from a different place. I traveled with her when she took a jagged rock and scratched the words "I still love you" into his front door. I have driven by his house with her in the middle of the night, night after night after night. She just sits outside his house and cries. And yet I know that humans must have their hearts broken before they can find their one and only. When I see her pain, I am glad that I am a house.

Some girls are afraid to be alone in Mexico, yet she visits me by herself often. She remembers the cold winter days when they would drink tea by the fire and make love on the floor. They would read books and laugh endlessly about nothing at all. In the middle of the night they would go outside naked to look at the stars. And now he's gone from her life. Except in her dreams that always come to an end too quickly. She knows it was his father who finally told him she was from a different place. For six generations their people had gone to the finest English schools. He was from another class. What hurt the most was that she knew he still loved her. She would wake up every morning at 4:00 A.M. without fail. She didn't know why, she just would. Then she would take her pen in hand, and the ink would be smeared by her tears.

Zen 149

I'm over you. I'll never think of you again. EVER! Except perhaps when I hear a child laugh, or hear a Chopin solo piano piece, or see a warm sunset, or hear a train, or see a black truck, or see green eyes, or hear seagulls, or see a teddy bear, or drink tea, or see a handmade sweater, or go to Mammoth, or have a drink of wine, or hear that stupid song, "Nothing compares to you." Otherwise, I'm over you!

The man was not strong enough to go against his father. She knew she was made of something that lasts, but why did it have to hurt so badly? God, if she could just go back in time and kiss his face just once, only once. She would make the kiss last forever, for he, and only he, made every room a universe.

I have seen surfers come and go. I watched the world champion do things with a wave that I had never seen before. I have seen the gringo residents set the cars of visiting surfers on fire. I have watched the dolphins play as the morning sky turned crimson-orange. I have watched a man quietly slip into the sea, never to return.

And I have seen friendships fail. Once a man let his friend fight two other men at once, while he continued to surf. The man could fight, though, and because he was righteous, he defeated his opponents and bent them to his will. Afterwards he never looked at the man who did not stand by his side again. Yes, sometimes their paths crossed. But the righteous man looked right through him, for he was just a shadow, a façade, a pretender.

I sit here on the cliff, my fireplace cold, the swells lulling me to sleep. Like a good dog, I wait for the sound of my loved one's car.

Through the barrier gate
We passed, with gay snowflowers
For our new attire!
                    -Kiyosuke

Children in the Sun

"You're the last of us."
"The good go first."
"It's okay. Really it is."
"You're inside me. You always will be."
"We rode to the snow."
"Discovered Mexico."

*   *   *

Derek's plan was simple. We'd go to the Thrifty drug and discount store and stuff gloves and beanies down our pants and up our jackets. Like some misdirected seventh graders, we knew how easy it was to steal. We got our goods and rode our trusty bikes home.

I asked my dad if I could leave the house just before sunrise to ride my bike to the snow. I was really surprised when he said yes, but that's how my dad was, unpredictable. We lived about 25 miles from the San Gabriel Mountains and the snow level was around 5000 feet. We met at Derek's house, having raided our refrigerators of all available food. It was 2:00 a.m.

We were an inseparable threesome, Derek, Zippy, and your host, Vincent. Derek was our leader. That's how it was. We had full backpacks with tools and water bottles taped to our bikes. We also carried patch kits and extra inner tubes for our Schwinn ten speeds. Into the darkness we steered up Azusa Blvd. By dawn we were at the base of the mountains. They looked so grand as the day filled with light. We suffered pedaling up those mountains. It was so cold and our cheap stolen gloves fell apart completely. Our food was gone by 10:00 a.m. We had about two and a half bucks combined. Yet Derek never stopped smiling and urging us upward. Sometimes we had to walk our bikes because of the steepness. At around 1:00 p.m. the wind really whipped up. The snow was still quite a ways off. A grandfather-type gentleman in a brown pickup pulled off in front of us and offered to throw the bikes in the back of his truck and haul us the rest of the way. Right away Zippy and I said yes.

Derek wouldn't hear of it. "Don't you guys get it? We're riding our bikes to the snow. If we take a lift, it will ruin it!" Before we could say anymore, Derek told the old guy, "Thanks, it's kind of you to offer, but we want to see if we can make it on our own."

About an hour later we made it to Crystal Lake and the beautiful snow. We shared a bowl of chile from the small snack bar. God, I can still taste it thirty-five years later. Zippy and I passed out on some benches, but Derek went off on one of his usual insane tree climbs. I couldn't even watch him when he climbed. He had absolutely no fear and would jump from branch to branch eighty feet off the ground. Thirty minutes later we sped down the hill as the sun and its warmth slid out of sight. The ride home was fine as long as it was down hill, but on the up hills and the flats, we were punished.

We arrived home around 11:30 p.m. My folks were so glad to see me alive that I didn't get in trouble. My father had been driving up and down the mountain looking for us. I lay down on my bed in all my clothes. Right before I went under my dad popped his head into my room.

He asked, "Tired, son?"

"Yeah, Dad."

"But it's a good tired, isn't it?"

"Yeah, Dad, it's a good tired."

*   *   *

Zippy's been dead for a few years now. He ended up getting caught in an avalanche, climbing in Alaska. Now Derek's dying, his mom and his love Mali leave us so we can talk. I wish I could be as brave as Derek; so unafraid. He's close to the edge now. Smiling like a son of a bitch. I touch his hair lightly and notice that my hand has caused many strands to fall out. I start crying. I hold back nothing; I'm free falling. A nurse walks in and turns around. Before she leaves, I see her big brown eyes are moist. She has dark hair, and her features are slightly Asian. She's a looker, and I know Derek has charmed her as he charmed all those who crossed his path. But I selfishly keep him to myself.

Derek whispers, "Don't cry for me, Vincent."

"Oh yeah, it's all about you, isn't it? You kook, I'm crying for me."

"I'm the one shitting himself." Derek laughs, and I hear the voice I've known for most of my life in his strained whisper. "The first Mexico trip, that was the one.

Zen 154

San Miguel spinning off its nut. Wave after bloody wave. We told our families we were going to San Onofre. Straight offshore all week." Then he said, "I'm cold, Vincent, really cold."

I take a blanket from the foot of his bed and pile it on the others. He continues, "We scammed Gemco for traveling money. We'd buy something really cheap, like a bag of manure. They'd put a big sticker on it that let the security guards know we paid for it. Then we'd send someone else in with the sticker hidden under their shirt. They'd put the sticker on a microwave or something and walk right on out. Then someone else would go in for a cash refund. We'd be fat with cash. I think we helped put them out of business. We all wore light-blue Converse high-tops; high school outcasts and proud of it. The jocks got the glory, but we knew who was really scoring. Tree caught some guys stealing our boards and we finally had to pull him off of them. Then there was the gorilla woman in Ensenada. We saw the Mexicans burn the preppies' car when they went to town. I didn't blame them. We drank tequila and Coronas; then drank some more. Dine and dash at the taco shop next to Hussongs; the cook chased us with a butcher knife for six blocks. We laughed and ran. Remember the Alpha Phi girls?" Then Derek looked at me with smiling eyes and softly did his Shakespeare thing: *"Golden lads and girls all must, as chimney-sweeps, come to dust."* He turned away and looked out the window as he continued. "That first week at San Miguel, that was our peak. We didn't know it. The speed of the wave that week, that cleansing speed. Rounding the jetty and screaming into the bay. Buying tamales from the kids in the morning, while the smell of burning trash floated down the valley. We flipped Zippy's bus; then flipped it upright. God watched over us. We were sure it would never end, we children in the sun."

Zen 155

I am awake.

-Buddha

You're All Talk

Wings sat in his old Ford truck looking out over the new swell. It was sunrise and he slowly enjoyed his first smoke of the day. Two guys out, he couldn't tell who they were since the break was so far out to sea, but he was pretty sure he knew them. Along this rugged stretch of coast there weren't many people he didn't know. He'd been shaping boards for thirty-five years, and he was proud that most of the strong surfers out his way rode his boards.

Wings suited up in his black wetsuit and slowly made his way down the cliff to his break. One of the magazines said you should never call a break your own. Morons. To call a break your own just meant it was your favorite place. It meant that you knew your break like you knew your woman, her moods, her secrets, her capabilities.

When he got to the bottom of the cliff, he was surprised to see another surfer there stretching. The surfer had an ultra-thin thruster, with airbrushed orange and yellow flames. His full wetsuit was also bright yellow. Wings figured the guy to be about his age, fifty.

Wings smiled and said, "Good morning."

The other surfer, whose hair was pure gray, looked at Wings with disgust, and replied, "Good until you showed up, longboarder."

Wings laughed and said, "I like all boards. Short or long, it doesn't matter to me. I surf them all."

Wings chuckled and climbed down the rocks and entered the water.

Gray Hair stood up, "Just don't call longboarding surfing!" He said with hatred and anger.

Wings stopped and looked at Gray Hair curiously. "What about the Duke? Wasn't that surfing?"

"That's my point." Fury was flying out of Gray Hair's mouth. "Surfing should be progressive, shorter not longer. Longboards are for fucking kooks!"

Wings smiled and said, "Whatever, brother, I don't know you from Adam. Peace be with you, I'm going surfing."

Gray Hair jumped up and down and screamed, "You're a GOON! You're a fucking KOOK! Fuck you, longboarder. Go home!"

For the first time Wings really looked at Gray Hair. He was a small man, much smaller than himself. Gray Hair's eyes burned with blue sparks. Wings could see that he loathed him with everything he had. Wings cocked his head sideways as if he were deciding what to do.

Then Wings said, "Okay." And walked out of the water, back up the rocks to Gray Hair. As soon as Wings approached him, Gray Hair started backing up fast, whimpering like a child.

Gray Hair blubbered, "You talk about peace. Yeah, it's always violence with your kind. Sure, violence is the answer. Don't you know anything but violence? Must it always come to violence? What about peace, my brother? Huh?"

Gray Hair's words threw Wings for a loop and he hesitated for a moment. During that moment Gray Hair scurried down to the water and paddled away from the cliff. As he paddled away, he yelled over his shoulder, "Fuck you! You're all talk. You're just fucking hot air. Suck my dick! Suck my dick, bitch!"

Zen 158

All at once the energy seemed to leave Wings. A great sadness overtook him. He thought, "This is why people quit surfing. This terrible feeling of dealing with blind hatred." He considered quitting surfing for the first time in his forty years of riding waves religiously. For a moment he thought about what his life would be like without surfing. Then a righteous anger arose inside him.

Wings yelled out from the bottom of his lungs, "ONLY GOD WILL JUDGE ME!" He slowly and methodically got into the water and paddled Gray Hair down. As Wings got close, Gray Hair stopped paddling and sat up on his tiny board to face him. When Gray Hair saw that Wings meant business, he tried to paddle away. Wing's career was shaping boards, and his body was solid and strong. He grabbed Gray Hair by his skinny ankle and pulled him close. Gray Hair tried to swing on Wings, but he grabbed his fists in mid-flight.

Wings looked at Gray Hair and said, "Are you serious? Is that it? That's your best shot? So I'm all talk, huh? You and your airbrushed board and yellow wetsuit. You want me to suck your dick, huh? I'm a bitch, huh?" Then he grabbed Gray Hair by the nape of his neck and pushed him off his board and under water. Gray Hair struggled, but he was at the mercy of Wings. He grabbed Wing's hair but Wings bit his wrist. Wings held him under until he was afraid he might kill him. Then he pulled him out of the water. Gray Hair's eyes were huge. Then Wings punched his nose, changing its shape.

Wings said, "You're just like an old man with a young woman: no matter what you do, you just look ridiculous. Don't come back to this beach until you learn some manners." He discarded Gray Hair like so much trash. Gray Hair paddled in defeated, and Wings paddled out and surfed with his friends, harder than ever.

Zen 159

We paddled out at Windansea
Windansea my secret lover
How I seek thee out in the obscure hours
You show me your wildest capabilities
Your naughty foam ball
Your emotional mood swings
Then, when the light comes you share yourself
with so many other men
Yet, I cannot stop loving you

My two-year-old son sat on the nose of my board
The surf was dark blue fun
It seemed so easy
We turned for two waves and missed them
Then, we really committed and I knew
that the wave was now in control
Oh, how grossly I misjudged the wave
I stood holding my son close
Yet, I could not squeeze him too tightly
Lest, like Lenny, I crush him. My son

I tell him in my happiest voice
"Hold on, Daddy loves you so much.
It's going to be okay,
hold on tight."
Instead of obliterating us
the ocean completely
and utterly surrounds us
Caressing us,
propelling us
My son is laughing
but I am so scared

Startled I awaken
Go to his crib
Pick him up
Hold him close

The Code

For Donnie

He grew up in a world where you simply did not let go of your board. This was a tradition handed down from the old days, before leashes, when a loose board was something to be avoided. He'd seen what a loose board could do. He'd avoided his fair share. It was a matter of honor.

On that last day, when it was really breaking, he felt strong and loose. The big waves seemed to slow down for him and let him paddle into them.

He shared a wave with his friend, the world champion, and told him, "That was the greatest wave of my life."

Then a large set came out of the deep north. He watched the wave come towards him, never taking his eyes off the peak. Instinctively he started inhaling through his nose and exhaling through his mouth. He paddled with everything he had, but he did not panic. He thought he had a good chance of duck-diving his big gun right through the base of the thickening peak. For just a moment he considered diving off his board and swimming as deep as he could to get under the biggest wave of the day. But there were surfers inside of him, and the code wouldn't allow him to pitch his board.

He stroked hard, and his paddle was strong and sure. There was no fear in his rhythm. He felt in control and, even as the wave began to lift him upwards and away, he never panicked. He'd been thrown over the falls before, and he knew he could take the beating. He gripped his prized gun with everything he had. He wrapped his arms and legs around the board.

The sun was out, and he was with his best friends. The weightlessness was not new to him. He'd felt it many times before. In that moment, just before the ocean knocked his soul clean out of his body, he knew he was part of something; part of the brotherhood of surfers. A brotherhood that was the only thing that really ever mattered to him. And then his spirit soared like a bird over the Pali and directly into the brilliance.

*To take to the sea
is to plunge into
heightened enlightenment.*

The Sharer

Keone dreamt that he was fighting his father. His father's grip was like an iron vice. For a moment Keone was paralyzed with fear. Then he remembered his father's weak spot. As he took control of the situation, all the air went out of his father as if he were a balloon. Keone woke up, sighed and thought, "Forgive him. Let him rest."

*　　　　　　*　　　　　　*

Keone arrived at the point at first light. The fog had come in pretty thick, and visibility was about forty yards. He could hear the surf thundering from the lookout spot. Drawing on the combination of his experience, Sean Collin's forecast, the high tide, and the lifeguard report, he was pretty sure it was double overhead, give or take a few feet. But the Point was a spot Keone knew well. The paddle out was easy enough and because of the way the Point sits, it rarely gets too critical. Keone suited up, stretched, had a smoke, and out he went.

He figured he'd sit on the boil and ride the inside bay. Keone took a few on the head on the way out. He always thought that taking a wave on the head was like the Zen Master hitting his student with a bamboo stick. The waves were like the teacher saying, "Wake up. Pay attention!" The swells were just like Keone knew they would be. A steep take off section with a long fun wall to follow. After Keone's first wave, something caught his attention as he paddled back out. He thought he saw another surfer in the mist riding the outside. Yes, he was almost sure he could see someone making beautiful carving turns along the dark walls. Keone was happy to see another surfer in the thick fog. He headed out to share the waves with him. As he went outside, the swells were really stacking up nicely. When a bomb came Keone's way he forgot about the other surfer and stroked into a dark blue drop. As the high tide backwash hit the incoming wave the angles met to create a wave of dreams, a churning spinning pocket that wanted to be ridden. A quarter mile later Keone kicked out and headed back through the fog. Keone caught glimpses of the other surfer in the mist. When the other surfed, the wave seemed to move according to his turns or vice versa. Yet Keone could never get close enough to talk to him. Soon the fog lifted, and the other surfer was gone. Keone assumed he had paddled way north, and had gotten out there. As the fog cleared, the crowd filled in. Keone surfed one in and wondered who the mystery carver was.

About a month later Keone woke up at 3:00 a.m. It was a full moon. When the moon was full it beckoned him. He looked out his window and the night looked like day. He softly kissed his wife and kids and drove to the ocean's edge. They would know that Daddy went surfing when they awoke.

At 3:30 a.m. Keone was on the rocks at the base of the Cliffs. The air had the smell of low-tide; a fishy mustiness. He lit up two slow-burning Duralogs and spaced them out about fifty feet apart. They served no purpose other than making Keone feel better. Later, at first light, Keone knew that other surfers would join him. Until then he would enjoy the head-high waves all by himself. Keone liked the night smells and the lights that were on, sprinkled up and down the coast. He paddled out and felt like a child stealing candy from an unlocked store. Under the moonlight the waves did their usual dance. Because the moon was towards the Western horizon, the waves were actually bands of darkness that did not reflect the moonlight on their approach. Yet, once up and riding the waves, he could see the reflection of the moonlight and enjoyed the experience to which he was addicted.

A set approached from the outside. There he was. The surfer that Keone had seen on the foggy day was out surfing now. He surfed right by Keone, and Keone gave a little hoot as the surfer swung his board in and around the curl. Then Keone caught a wave and rode by the other surfer as he paddled out. The other surfer hooted, too. The waves just kept coming and they were in a fine rotation. They never even spoke to one another for they were too busy riding waves. Keone wanted to introduce himself to the other surfer, but as the first light of day approached, the other surfer paddled south and out of sight. He was gone.

Keone told no one else about the other surfer. He was glad there was someone else out there that needed the water as he did. A few days later the swell of the winter was upon San Diego, and Keone knew that the spot for him was Little Makaha. Because of family obligations, Keone didn't paddle out until afternoon. The wind had come up pretty good from the north, but Little Makaha is so far out to sea that a north wind blows offshore on the cloud break waves. Keone pulled up his Jeep and saw that there was one person surfing. Little Makaha breaks about a mile from the rocks in the North Bird area of La Jolla. Keone could just barely see another surfer carving the outside lefts. The lefts ledged up four times the height of the rider, barn-like. Keone knew it was the fluid surfer from the fog and moonlight. He suited up, stretched, had his smoke, and off he went.

The paddle out to Little Makaha takes about thirty minutes. There's a long stretch of white-water and when you are under water you can hear the ocean rumble. All one can do is put his head down and dig. After what seemed like a hundred duck-dives Keone made it out and paddled right up to the surfer. The other surfer looked a lot like Keone: dark, thinning hair, a long gun, and a big smile.

The surfer glanced at Keone and said, "It's fun, huh?" Then he paddled towards an approaching set. They surfed alone for hours. The left at Little Makaha is a blue water wave that seems to break in slow motion. It's a perfect long wall that allows boards to hit their maximum speed. Keone felt good, he paddled into the biggest waves he could find. Just having the other surfer out there with him gave him confidence.

Two other surfers paddled out towards the close of day. Keone had had enough fun and decided not to press his luck. He took one all the way in. He didn't know what happened to his surfing partner. As he walked up the stairs, he saw his friend Pier looking at the waves through binoculars.

"You going out?" Keone asked.

"No, I surfed San Miguel for five hours this morning. It was rocking, I'm toast."

"Did you see that guy ripping out there? I don't know who he is, but he's all over it," Keone said.

"What are you talking about? I've been watching you carving through my biney's for an hour. There's two guys out there now, but you were all alone." Then Pier snorted out a laugh and said, "Sixties flashback, huh?" He resumed his lookout.

Lo! as the wind is, so is mortal life:
A moan, a sigh, a sob, a storm, a strife.
-Sir Edwin Arnold 1892

The Paddle

When Keone read *Into the Wild,* he could relate to the protagonist Chris. He told his wife, "If you want to understand me, read this book."

She replied, "I'll never understand you, but I love you."

Keone had the need that trekkers and climbers have. The need to be near the edge every so often. He was careful enough. Though he was an experienced waterman, he knew there was always the potential for something going just a little wrong. But that's what scratched his constant itch.

Keone left work early one day because he heard some bigger fish were showing on the outside. He asked another teacher to cover his sixth period class. He took off his watch and drove down to the beach. He hated wearing a watch and only wore one at work.

The launch from Simmons Reef was always easy on the small days. He was going to wear his spring suit since the water had warmed up, but at the last minute he put on his full suit. In the back of his mind a small voice said, "You never know if you'll have to spend the night out there."

Clouds were moving in. He paddled out on his fishing board around 2:00 p.m. The ocean was sheet glass. Within ten minutes he was at the kelp bed. Then began the strenuous task of pulling his twelve-foot board through the 100 yards of thick kelp. Strapped on his inter-island windsurfing board was a red milk crate. In the corners of the crate were pieces of p.v.c. piping wired in to hold his fishing poles. In the kelp bed he came upon spaces of clear water that he knew held healthy calicos, but today he was heading to the outside, where the commercial boats fished. The barracuda had made their spring debut, and Keone wanted to brush up for the Summer Windansea Boardfishing Tournament.

By 3:00 p.m. Keone was on the outside. The wind was rising quickly out of the southeast. Clouds continued to fill the sky. He paddled up current of the New Seaforth, a ninety footer out of Mission Bay. He drifted back around the boat's chum-line and caught and released two barracudas in the 30-inch range. He was throwing black and green fish-traps, and they seemed to be doing the trick.

There was a strong north current that, combined with the southeast wind, kept Keone quite busy. The New Seaforth started its engine, pulled anchor, and headed home. Just then Keone hooked up with something that started spooling his Penn Jigmaster 500 reel, which held 300 yards of new pink thirty-pound test line. Keone focused on catching the fish. He noticed that the ocean was turning ugly and the wind had picked up alarmingly out of the Southeast. Rain was beginning to fall, yet Keone knew he must catch this fish. It started to pull his board into the wind. Water splashed over the board, soaking Keone and his gear. Keone wanted this fish to take home to show to his daughter, Stormy, and his son, Tiger. For if he arrived home after fishing without a fish, there would be disappointment. Because Keone was focused entirely on the fish, time slipped by. The fish didn't fight like a barracuda, which would shake its head in small, quick yanks. Nor did it fight like a yellowtail that would pull with one strong, steady pull. No, this was like a heavy weight that was alive. Keone was pretty sure he had his holy grail, a big white sea bass. He also knew that the wind was blowing him out to sea and north. He saw a commercial boat coming out of the north, heading for Mission Bay. For a moment he thought of cutting his line and intercepting the boat so he could ask for a ride in. He knew he wouldn't be denied, given the deteriorating conditions. But the fish was closer now, and when it saw the board it made a final hard run. Keone decided, against a strong inner voice, that he would catch this fish, then overpower the ocean itself to paddle in. He thought, "This must be what the climbers call 'summit fever.' They lose their good sense in the hopes of achieving something great. That's what sometimes kills them. Well, I've been hunting this fish for a long time."

He had been fighting the fish for over an hour when he felt it weakening. Finally, he was able to slowly gain line on the brute. By now he guessed he was six or seven miles offshore. He thought he saw the weather buoy between him and the land, but the light was fading and he couldn't be sure. Then the white sea bass rose to the surface. "The fish of a lifetime," whispered Keone. He used his small gaff to stick the fish. He knew the best place to gaff a fish was in the head. You didn't corrupt the meat, the fish would bleed less, and you might speed up the dying process. He lifted the head of the fish out of the water and was surprised by its weight. He guessed the fish weighed over sixty pounds, and it was far from dead. It thrashed about but Keone put all of his two hundred and ten pounds on the fish, lying right on top of it, trapping it against the board until, little by little, the life of the fish faded away. The fish drowned in the air. It was quickly getting dark.

Out loud he said, "Thank you for your life, fish. I will nourish my family with your flesh." He used bungy cords and fishing line to fasten the fish in the milk crate. Its head stuck far out one side, and its tail hung far out the other. The sun was well gone, and the moon tried to break out of the stormy clouds. The wind now howled out of the southeast, pushing waves up and over the top of Keone's board. He paddled deep, setting his body towards the rear of the board. He could not find a rhythm. Keone was feeling like a fool. He stroked harder and deeper, but he could not make headway. Everything he had, he poured into his motion for 60 minutes straight. He had left a note for his wife saying he would be home at 8:30 p.m. He began to wonder if he'd get home at all.

"I'm a fucking idiot! I'm a FUCKIIIIIIIING IDIOT!" he shouted to the sky. But he never did stop paddling. Hunger ripped at his stomach. He had an apple in his milk crate, and there was the fish. But he would not eat the fish. No, he must take it home to show his children.

Thoughts flowed. "Me. Big fucking hunter. Big fucking waterman. I'm a fucking kook. I'm the most selfish son of a bitch in the world. What kind of father am I? What a dumbshit. I quit. Nowhere to go. No one to take my place. I'm heading out to sea. First my brother, now me. Two lost to the sea. Who would have thought? I'm alive. I'm dead. I'm a husband, go figure. Daddy, Jesus, Abba, Abba, Abba." Then he grabbed his apple and tore into it, paddling with one hand and devouring with the other. He twisted his body to torque the board against the current, the wind, and the waves. The apple gave him renewed strength.

He had been battling his way shoreward for five hours when he finally found his rhythm. He had turned a bit downwind and was heading further north. By hesitating a microsecond between each stroke, he was able to slide down the backside of a steady wind-chop. He felt himself making progress. He knew he must make it to the kelp because the southeast wind sometimes roared loudest in the middle of the night. His arms were heavy. He felt something slam the bottom of his board very hard. Then the board was lifted well out of the water. His bowels emptied and he gripped the board and closed his eyes. In his mind he saw a Great White with a big, beat-up red nose. He could not chase the Great White out of his mind, but he knew he could live with this thought. It was not a new one. He shook for over thirty minutes. Then he resumed paddling.

*   *   *

By now Keone figures it's around 1:00 a.m. He doesn't want to think about what his wife and kids are going through. He's pretty sure his kids are asleep and don't even know he's missing. Keone knows that there are people out looking for him. His wife would have called a man she hated before she called anyone else. She loathed him because he was a terrible husband to her friend and a terrible father to their children. But she also knows that no one knows the sea like he does. Keone kept looking about the sea for boats, but the visibility was next to nothing and he knew a boat wouldn't see him unless it ran over the top of him. The wind and current are making him bleed for every inch. Keone knows that his strength is not without end. If the wind increases anymore, he won't be even able to paddle, he'll just have to hang on to his board. Every mile he's swept out will decrease 100-fold the chance he'll be found at night. By morning he'll be so far out to sea that rescue on a surfboard in the big ocean isn't a slam-dunk. He digs into his deepest reserves and starts laughing.

He whispers, "The Shackleton expedition." Some how this makes him giggle more and he remembers a song from his favorite childhood TV show, "Davey and Goliath." It beats to a choo-choo train rhythm and says, "All alone, all alone," then goes "God is with you, God is with you…All alone, all alone, all alone, all alone, God is with you God is with you…"

There's no such thing as time now. Keone's world is a ceaseless paddle. His body is torqued from his toes to the top of his head. The moon now breaks out of the clouds and the rain stops, but the ocean is fire and brimstone. Keone paddles. It's hard to tell if he's making headway.

Quitting is not an option. He knows he'll paddle until he's dead. He thinks of the many insects and unwanted pet fish he's flushed down the toilet. That's how he feels, like a small life being flushed down a giant toilet. Yet, he believes he's making progress. The lights of the shoreline seem to be getting closer. Then he thinks he detects a softening of the wind. It loosens up the last of his reserves. He knows now he's tapping into something he's never used before. Keone feels his body feeding off itself. He's no longer human, just an animal, scratching for his life. He guesses the time is around three or four. He wants to get to his family, but his arms are no longer listening to his commands very well. Then he feels the kelp under his board. Is it a stray piece? No, it's the paddy. He fights his way into the thick of the kelp because he knows if he gets deep enough no wind will pull him out.

"Thank you, master of the universe," he whispers and puts some kelp into his mouth and chews and swallows and there is no bottom to his stomach. But he cannot rest because he knows his family is frantic. His arms don't want to listen. He implores them but they refuse. He wraps kelp around and around his arms and legs and closes his eyes as the wind settles down. In the back of his mind he thinks he hears a helicopter. But his mind will no longer wake-up. He falls deep into the crevice of exhaustion.

He doesn't know if he's slept or not. But sleep or rest, it's the same. He does know that his arms are now listening. He realizes time has gone by. There's the sound of a boat but it's offshore. The night is now giving way to the first hint of daylight. Keone pulls himself through the kelp bed. It's long and punishing work. Then he's free of the kelp-bed and heading towards shore. The planet is filling with light. The ocean is calm and the waves are small. He thinks he's well north of Torrey Pines and he realizes he's almost to Cardiff Reef. He paddles onto the rocky beach. There's morning traffic on Pacific Coast Highway.

He drags his board well up on the cobblestones and sees a parking lot just north. He starts walking very slowly for his legs are weak and his balance is off. Then he starts walking faster as the thought of hearing his wife's voice pulls him forward. He begins a slow trot now and his body is responding. Then he's sprinting for all he's worth towards a phone in the lonely parking area. He's running faster than he's ever run before. The phone is broken.

He goes up to an older surfer suiting up in the parking lot and says, "I've been out to sea all night and I'd like to call my wife. Do you have a cell phone I can use, please?"

The man looks at him for just a moment. He studies Keone's eyes, then says, "Sure."

Keone's calls his house. His wife answers the phone. She's crying. Keone is crying too. His first words are, "Tell the kids I caught a white sea bass."

Zen 175

Zen does not confuse spirituality with thinking about God while one is surfing. Zen spirituality is just to go surfing.

Hunters and Gatherers

Jimmy always tries to reason with irrational surfers. He might say, "What happened to you that you're so full of hate? Where's your aloha? Surfing should be fun. Did your mother or father abandon you when you were young? I'd kill myself if I was as angry as you." And so on. But many simply can't be reasoned with. They want a fight, and they won't settle for anything less.

There's a switch in Jimmy's mind, and a giant hand hovers over it. The hand won't flip the switch unless it has to. Jimmy has it down pretty pat. In one way or another, he'll say, "You can always try and kick my ass." On four occasions in the last twenty years he's been taken up on his offer. Then the hovering giant hand flips the switch, and there's no turning back. Twice he walked away laughing, completely unscathed. Once he woke up in the hospital with a concussion and a broken nose and arm. Now I'll tell you about the most recent time someone tried to kick Jimmy's ass.

Jimmy believes that on the day he was born a shark also was born. The shark and he share the same Pacific Ocean. He knows that one day the shark will try to eat him. It's inevitable. Jimmy first met the shark off the east end of Catalina when he was sixteen years old. Jimmy and his brothers got four hooks into it from four different poles. The angry shark cart-wheeled right out of the water, incredibly high, going end over end until it had snapped all four metal leaders. After it was free, it swam right by the boat, getting a good look at the fishermen.

The next time Jimmy crossed paths with this fish was when he was twenty-one years old, surfing at Kauai's Tunnels in post-sunset emptiness. My how the fish had grown. Jimmy saw the shark, and he lucked into a wave and raced to the exposed reef. Jimmy rode his board right onto the reef and waited there, being washed back and forth. He knew he should wait longer, but it was already dark; so after about half an hour, he just hit the deep water and made the long paddle across the bay to the cool sand.

He surfs at night or in the lonely fog. He likes to fish from his surfboard, solitary miles offshore. He knows the shark is coming, but he thinks he's immortal until God takes him home. He loves Vixen Reef, though he wouldn't recommend you go surfing there. There are lots of other less technical waves where you'll have more fun. When he goes there, he sits right offshore. It's his way of not dealing with the outside crowd and getting consistent rides, albeit fin-grinders. He's paid his dues at Vixen Reef. He never drops in on anybody and he's quietly polite. He has friends there he respects tremendously. But no matter where he's surfing up and down the coast, every once in a while someone's going to spout off. Perhaps it's in a hunter's nature to occasionally engage.

Late in the summer Jimmy headed out for a mid-week, mid-morning , Vixen Reef go-out. The tide was funky so the crowd was down. That's pretty much Jimmy's M.O. He surfs spots on the off-tide to get away from crowds. He was going to try out a new board that a guy named Spock reshaped for him. He took an old, sinking gun of Jimmy's and stripped it down and reshaped it into a fun board.

As Jimmy walked down the beach he heard someone screaming from the parking lot. He looked up and saw three men looking his way and pointing. Jimmy simply cannot surf if there is any negative energy directed his way. It totally ruins it for him, and he can't relax until the issue is addressed. Jimmy knew they were yelling at him.

They were really making a scene with one particular guy starting to get excited, shouting. "Is that Spock's logo? Did Spock shape that board? He's a fucking kook, he can't shape; that board sucks."

Jimmy set down the board, fins up, and walked up the small hill to the parking lot. As he got closer he recognized one of the guys as someone he had fought once, a long time ago at Black Rock. The guy whispered something to the others and walked away quickly. Jimmy was pretty sure he wasn't coming back. Then the other guy walked away, towards the houses, leaving the guy who had been yelling the loudest standing there defiantly. He looked about Jimmy's size, six two, around 210 pounds or so. He was over thirty, unshaven, and it appeared as if he might have slept in his clothes. He also had a pretty big nose. Jimmy walked up to him getting within perhaps 10 feet of him.

Jimmy said, "What's with all your yelling?"

"That's Spock's label, isn't it? He's a fucking kook, that board's a piece of shit, Spock is a piece of shit."

"Listen," Jimmy said, "I'm not sure what your problem is with Spock. He shaped me this board out of an old gun and only charged me for materials, so he's all right by me. I can't enjoy my session with you out here yelling."

The big-nosed guy came back, "I'm educated, man, I know my rights. I have the freedom of speech and I can yell all I want and you can't stop me." He was getting heated up, and the sleeping hand in Jimmy's head was stirring.

Jimmy said, "Why don't you tell Spock how you feel? He's here almost every sunset. Save your anger for him, not for me."

Big Nose's breathing was becoming heavier and his eyes were fastened on Jimmy. For some reason the words "Punch him in the throat" were beginning to drift lazily into Jimmy's mind. Big Nose started yelling, making a big scene, "But you're a kook if you're riding his boards. They don't fucking work. He's a kook, and you're a kook, and you are OUT OF HERE!" He pointed inland with one hand and balled his other hand into a fist. He took a few steps towards Jimmy.

This is what Jimmy expected all along. From the first time Big Nose yelled at him across the beach, Jimmy knew he would have to be dealt with. The finger in Jimmy's head calmly rested on the switch. He un-weighted his left foot very slightly and turned just a bit away from Big Nose. He liked the feeling. He wasn't scared at all. This was just a sparring match for him. No matter how bad Big Nose was, Jimmy knew he was up to it. He was up to anything. He had been trained by the Sand Man and the Sand Man knew how to teach the art of street fighting.

Jimmy smiled his most sincere smile and very softly said, "Chase me out."

Big Nose gave it some serious thought, he really did. At this point Jimmy was detached from himself and the choice was all Big Nose's. Then Big Nose relaxed.

He said, "My name is Whitey. I'm sorry I yelled at

Zen 180

you. I respect you for walking up here." He held out his hand for an island handshake and as Jimmy shook it, he thought Whitey might be sincere. He continued, "It's nothing to do with you. You're right I should focus my anger on Spock. He gives the kids on the inside crap. Can you imagine? He hassles little kids. They're our future. His designs simply don't work. He's so stupid he doesn't even know it." As he turned to look at the sea, Jimmy recognized him for the first time. This was a guy Jimmy had surfed the Cave with on many serious days. With the Cave it's all or nothing. And Jimmy remembered that one particularly shifting, heaving big day this guy was crawling into some deep dark holes. Not only that, but he remembered there were a few young high school boys trying to scratch over the edge and he was cheering them on. He really cared about the kids.

Jimmy told him, "Whitey, you and I have surfed a lot of days together." Whitey looked at Jimmy again, studying him, then smiled, "You ride white guns right? Where's your goatee?" Jimmy was glad he remembered him and he told him he'd seen him air dropping some good ones. Whitey squatted down and grabbed a dirt clod to draw a diagram on the parking lot.

He said, "Here's the Cave. There's a knuckle out there where the wave will let you in really early." He wasn't telling Jimmy anything he didn't know, but Jimmy was glad he was sharing what he thought was special information.

Then he asked, "Isn't that board kind of gunny for today?"

Jimmy told him, "Money's kind of tight. It's the only rider I've got right now."

He smiled and said, "I'll give you a board. I know all about being broke."

Jimmy wasn't completely surprised. When he lived

in Hawaii, he and his friends often gave boards to one another. Jimmy believed that surfboard giving was something that could only be learned in Hawaii. Some people made fun of the end of "Big Wednesday" when Matt gave his board to the kid who told him, something like, "Dude, that was the most radical ride I've seen in my life." But Jimmy saw that as something beautiful and natural. Matt had come back from the dead; it was time for him to pass on the magic.

Then Whitey said, "I'll get you a board right now." He started looking around, and Jimmy realized he was going to steal someone's board for him.

Jimmy told him, "I don't need a new board, Whitey. I'm good for now." Then Whitey sat on a bench overlooking the beach and began his story.

His voice was quiet, "Spock and I went to U.C.S.B. together. The difference was I had to audit the engineering courses. So while these rich bozos sat in classes saying stupid things, I couldn't even speak my mind because I wasn't a paying customer. All Spock's life he's had a silver spoon in his mouth. I'm ten times the engineer he is. I was an orphan. No parents to take care of me, no sir. I've been taking care of myself all my life. Spock's had every advantage and he still can't make a board that functions. His shapes are a joke. His stupid boards aren't worth crap. You know he charged a Japanese surfer $500.00 for a new custom?"

Jimmy told him, "Yeah, but that Japanese guy is used to paying $1,500.00 for a custom so he thinks he scored. Spock's an artist; I like his work. Time for me to surf now, Whitey, I'll see you at the Cave."

But then the two guys who had split returned with a third guy. The third guy was a Rockabilly: big Elvis sideburns, hair dyed black, Stray Cat tattoos on his large biceps. He walked right up to Jimmy and, without a word, tried to punch his lights out. Jimmy jumped back, barely out of the punch's range, and then the switch in his head went *on*. "Four on one? Right on!" yelled Jimmy. He laughed, bringing his arms up, moving on his tiptoes in a slow wide circle. In his mind he went back in time, to the Sand Man's studio.

From the time Jimmy was eight years old he lived next to a martial arts studio. His family didn't have the money for him to work out there, but he hung around. He did odd jobs sweeping, cleaning windows, answering the phone, cleaning the bathroom, whatever work the Sand Man wanted done. In exchange he was allowed to join the classes. He worked his way up over the years until he earned his instructor's belt, then his black belt. It wasn't the kind of studio that went to tournaments. The Sand Man said they were bullshit. The Sand Man believed there was only one way to become a strong fighter. And that way was FULL-CONTACT sparring. One on one, two on one, three on one, four on one, five on one, six on one, two on two, three on three, and any variation the Sand Man could dream up. Lights out, hands tied, two guys tied by the wrist, blindfolds, the Sand Man was always creative. They worked out with all sorts of weapons: staffs, knives, guns, swords, throwing stars, baseball bats, chairs, and chains. And every night, after every work out, the Sand Man would punch you in the gut, lifting you off the ground. It could hurt like hell, but you couldn't show it, and it made you harder.

Jimmy said, "I like the strong quiet type. No wasting time." All four converged on Jimmy, but he went straight for the Rockabilly who seemed to have a little speed. Jimmy moved in, took one to his face and landed a solid right solar-plex punch on the Rockabilly. The Rockabilly fell on the hood of a VW wagon. Someone jumped on Jimmy's back and he dropped an elbow into their gut and dropped his right fist into their crotch. He heard a howl and turned around to see Big Nose in a ball, holding his nuts.

Jimmy said, "Always protect the family jewels!"

One of the guys did a leg sweep on Jimmy, and he went down hard but sprang right back up. Two guys rushed in and tried to take Jimmy down. They got in a good couple of punches, but he used his knees and elbows to hurt them.

As they hit the ground Jimmy said, "Not so close, I hardly know you." The Rockabilly was back in the game, coming in quick. He threw up a high kick and Jimmy grabbed his foot in the air and threw it into the sky.

Jimmy said, "Don't leave your kick up there hanging!" The Rockabilly's feet went up over his head and he landed on his dyed black hair smack on the pavement. Meanwhile, Big Nose came in swinging and Jimmy took a few to his ribs before he dropped him, once and for all, with a crunching head butt.

Jimmy said, "Don't leave your face unprotected!" Then added, "You guys are pretty good," so they wouldn't feel so bad.

His nose and knuckles were bleeding, and he was sore, but he couldn't remember the last time he had so much fun. He kicked one of them hard between the legs and then, without putting his foot back on the ground, he stomped the back of the same guy's head as he folded over.

Jimmy heard a siren, then a cop rolled into the lot. Jimmy was standing and there were four guys around him, slowly getting to their feet.

A big, black cop got out of his car, fat nightstick in hand, and said, "What's going on, gentlemen?"

Jimmy laughed and said, "Just boys having fun officer, just boys having fun."

*There is in the world only one
figure of
absolute beauty: Christ.*

-Dostoyevsky

Ghosts

Last week I went for a surf in the late afternoon at Imperial Beach. The wind was blowing hard onshore as it does most afternoons. It was blown out, but plenty punchy. There was no one surfing as far as the eye could see. As I was stretching on the beach, I saw a woman and two children make their way across the sand. Winter was here and it was getting cold. The kids were just wearing thin t-shirts and they were way underdressed. There was a boy about four and a girl about three. They came close to me so they could check out my board. The little boy looked at me as if I had some fantastic secret or something. Their mom sat off alone, looking like she was in trouble.

I asked her, "Are you all right?"

She was about thirty-five or so, dressed in clothes I knew were expensive. No question, she was a head turner.

She looked at me and said in an uneven voice, "No, I'm not all right. Why do you ask?"

Her response was sincere. I said, "Because it's way too cold for your kids to be out here in those clothes, they'll get sick for sure."

"I know," she replied, "I just needed a little time on the beach to think."

I imagined that perhaps she was in an abusive marriage or maybe she was broke, I didn't know. I had a little money in my car, or I thought that perhaps my church could help her.

I asked, "Do you need a little money?"

She sort of giggled and said, "No, I wish the problem was only money. We have a ranch out towards Jamul. It's haunted. There are old Indian spirits that are in my home, poltergeists. My kids and I have seen them. My husband doesn't believe me. It's easy for him; he works in L.A. and only comes home on weekends. But they're there and they're angry. Forgive me for pouring out my soul but it's easier to talk to a stranger." I didn't doubt her story. Not so much that I believed there were demons there, but I believed she believed they were there.

I told her, "Your husband doesn't believe you because they are not real to him. These are *your* demons. I fought demons once. It took a long time for me to win. It's not a battle that is won quickly or easily."

She said, "I feel better talking to you, but I can tell you want to get in the water. Just answer me this: did the demons go away?"

I replied, "Actually, I know they'll never completely be gone. But my God is so powerful that I can just turn my back on them and walk away. I'll pray for you, and I suggest you pray too. There is no demon that can stand up to Christ." And then I went alone into the stormy, vast ocean.

Vanished now
in water
this wake
where a
moment ago
I turned
my surfboard

Surfing to Ground Zero

September 11:

At 7:15 in the morning I arrived at my classroom at Southwest High School. My neighbor teacher is an ex-Air Force pilot who flew in Vietnam; he asked me if I'd heard we are under attack.

He said, "Terrorists just flew two birds into the World Trade Center, one into the Pentagon, and there's one down in Pennsylvania. This is it, baby, we're at war." He then quickly walked away, and I turned on my classroom TV.

During second period my principal, John DeVore, came into my room. I was standing in front of the TV.

He had a clipboard in his hand and said, "Greg, I need you to teach an art class for me. It will mean one less U.S. History class, but I need your help here." Just then the second tower fell down. I watched the TV, stunned.

John didn't even look up, he asked me again, "Will you take the art class? I could really use your help."

I replied, "John, the world's falling apart before our

eyes and you're worried about the master schedule?"

"I can do something about the master schedule; I can't do anything about that," he nodded towards the TV. Just then the seed of a thought was planted. I could do something about New York though I didn't know what.

"Yes, John, I'll teach the art class."

As John walked briskly out of the classroom I knew what the word "focus" truly meant. If I worked for a million principals, I would never work for one as great as John DeVore. He was driven, and nothing, not even war, was going to divert him from his path. In just three years I watched him turn the worst school in the district into the best, an amazing feat that required everything he had. No matter how early I got to school, no matter how late I left, John was there. He expected nothing less than the best we had to give and his office door was never closed. I love teaching U.S. History. We're looking at the founding of the country, and it's quite timely. You may recall that our Declaration of Independence ends with the following sentence, "And for support of this Declaration, with a firm reliance on the protection of divine Providence, we mutually pledge to each other our Lives, our Fortunes, and our sacred Honor." I have tried to be as strong as I can be so the students aren't alarmed. I explained that at one time in history the world was petrified of pirates. They ran the seas and oceans and were fierce fighters who were not afraid to die. But the civilized worlds united and waged war against the pirates, deleting a vast majority of them.

For most of my adult life I have hung on to the words of Jesus Christ, Mohandas Gandhi, and Martin Luther King. Gandhi believed that if we took an eye for an eye we would all be blind. And yet, when I look at my own children, I know this dark evil must be rooted out. Of the Revolutionary War Thomas Paine wrote, "These are the times that try men's souls." As it was, it is.

Zen 190

September 14:
I didn't paddle out for three days. I just raced home after work everyday to be with my family. My wife finally convinced me to go for a surf. I went out at Little Point. The tide was wrong but the swell was on the rise. I knew that one or two waves from every set would be rideable, if I sat wide. Sometimes I need to surf alone; this was one of those times. These last few years I have become successful at finding empty breaks. Sometimes they're mushy and sometimes they're shallow. I started thinking of the firemen's families. I pictured my family going to bed if I had been suddenly taken from them. I tried to imagine my wife holding and soothing our children. I let the pain out then realized I must try and get to New York City.

I didn't tell my wife right away. I called my friend Terry Rodgers, the Coastal Issues writer for the San Diego Union Tribune. I love Terry. Perhaps it's because we both have lost brothers to the mist. Perhaps it's his fierce love for his son and wife. There have been times in my life when I have met certain humans with whom I have felt immediately at home. They have had a deep vibration in their voice that assured me they could be trusted. Terry is one of these people. Terry not only writes cleanly about surfers, but he also can hold his own on a big day at Sunset Cliffs. We've ridden winter swells together under the full moon at Swamis. I trusted him and asked him if he had any inside information on possible terrorist activity here in San Diego. He said he knew of none, and his feeling was that we should be all right. I then invited him to join me on my trip to New York. He liked the idea, but he couldn't get away from work. He told me he'd keep an eye out for anybody who might be interested in driving there with me.

September 16:
I told my wife I was leaving for New York on the 18[th,] alone, in my car. I'd take our Honda wagon and sleep

in it. At first she was stunned, then angry.

She said, "Before you go off in search of whatever it is you're looking for, you'd better remember you're a father now. What if something happens to you? You look like a terrorist."

I said, "I'll shave."

"There are 140,000 miles on your car, and it needs tires," she said.

"It will make it," I answered.

"We have no money."

"I'll charge it all. I'm going."

"It's not safe to drive cross country alone right now. I know you're going because you say you are. Just do me one favor, find someone to go with you."

I said, "Okay."

Then she held me close and told me, "I'm not surprised you want to go there." Ain't love grand?

I felt certain I could find someone who would be willing to hop in my car and go. I was going to pay for the trip on our Visa. I know two very passionate U.S. History teachers, but they both passed without a second thought. The airlines were flying again. I kept looking high and low for a driving partner, but it wasn't happening. I asked my pastors, newspaper writers, fellow teachers, some professors from S.D.S.U. and even some perfect strangers. I couldn't find one other person who shared my compulsion to get to New York City.

September 22:

My wife's been home with the kids now for over three years. We love it and wouldn't have it any other way. Money is tight. We don't mind. I decided to try to raise the money to fly. I checked first with my district. In education we're forever hammered with the words, "teachable moments." I thought perhaps my district would send me out there so I could report back. No go.

Zen 192

The superintendent said, "No one in this district is flying anywhere."

I tried soul organizations who have supported me in the past: The California Teachers Association, Donna Frye's office, the Friends of Rollo Fishing Organization, ABC News San Diego, The Union-Tribune, Reef Brazil, The Surfrider Foundation, Western Outdoor News, South Swell, Surfdog Records, Pacific Beach Taco Surf. No go. These people are the BEST in the world, but business had spiraled downward everywhere. I was getting discouraged. I contemplated just putting the whole thing on the Visa, but we had worked so hard to get out of debt that I decided I just couldn't do it to my wife and family. I started to think that perhaps it wasn't going to happen.

October 10:

Then my church, Paseo Del Rey, said they'd be good for $200.00, and right away Steve Pezman said he'd be good for an additional $200.00. David Gray of Huck-Fin Fishing Association then came through with $100.00. I also had $100.00 hidden away in my wetsuit fund. My students knew what I was working towards, and every day they would ask if I was going to New York. I began to realize they were helping to fuel my desire to go. Somehow I would be going for them too. I hung some small paintings in the teacher's lounge at my school. When teachers heard I was using the money to go to New York, I quickly sold $250.00 worth. I started making calls back to New York to find out if any of the fallen firemen surfed. In California a fair percentage of firemen are surfers. That's when I first heard about fireman Steve "Bells" Belson, Steve was a lifelong passionate surfer who lived on Rockaway Beach. He was a lifeguard who became a fireman. I began a phone correspondence with Steve's friend and fellow fireman Brian Thomas. It was difficult connecting with the fireman by phone, as I taught by day and every night he went to a different funeral or memorial.

October 25:

Through an article by Outdoor Writer Ed Zieralski of the San Diego Union Tribune, I hooked up with Chuck Robinson of Fish for America. Chuck had collected and sent over 6,000 pounds of fresh-frozen fish to feed the workers at Ground Zero. He bought a couple of studies from me for $150.00 but, more importantly he offered to get me some work feeding the workers. That was it. I bought my ticket.

October 31:

This morning before school, a fellow teacher came up to me and said, "Here, I want to give this to you for your trip." It was $15.00. Somehow his gesture broke down the last of my defenses. I went to my empty classroom to think about things.

November 2:

I decided to pack as lightly as possible with everything in my backpack.

As I said goodbye to my family, my little girl Stormy started crying hysterically, "What if you get killed, what if you get killed?" I held her precious, beautiful face between my hands and kneeled in front of her, our noses almost touching.

I told her, "I promise you, I'm coming home. I promise you! I'll call you tomorrow morning from New York. I'll call you every morning and every night." It didn't reassure her, and my wife had to hold her back as I left the house.

I drove out to Ontario Airport for my Jet Blue red-eye flight. I was a little nervous boarding the plane, but the crew's laughter helped me relax. We landed at J.F.K. as the sun rose. I stood up while we were taxiing and people around me got very uncomfortable so I sat down quickly.

November 3:

I took a shuttle to Bouley Bakery at West Broadway and Duane. I saw more police than I had ever seen before. Every street was lined with New York's finest. Bouley Bakery provides food for the Red Cross, which passes it along to the workers at Ground Zero. It's a hectic place, and it took me a few minutes to find someone who could talk to me. Then I met the shift supervisor, and he asked for two picture I.D.s. He wanted to know whom I knew. I appreciated how careful they were being. He told me they were good for a few hours and to check in at 1:00 p.m. for the next shift. I walked out, looked right, and saw a big building that was black with every window blown out. I headed towards it. With the time difference, it was too early to call my daughter.

It looked as though a giant had thrown a temper tantrum. Pieces of buildings were ripped away. Smoke was pluming upwards in ever-changing directions. I walked the perimeter. There was a huge green screen, perhaps twenty feet high that completely surrounded Ground Zero. I came upon the firemen's memorial section. I had brought some flags made by my daughter and our local Cub Scouts. I put them on a huge pile of teddy bears. Then I started reading the memorials looking for something about Steve Belson.

Perhaps the one I'll remember most was a poster board written by a young hand. It said, "Mommy's sick. Daddy, please come home. We've been waiting over a month now. We hoped you were in a hospital. Please come home, every time I think of you I start crying. Come home now. I miss you VERY VERY much. And if you're in heaven please watch over all of us because we're not doing too good." There were hundreds of pictures of families together. Photos of happy people in Halloween costumes, at dances, and holiday gatherings, amusement parks, and so on. So very many smiling faces in the photos. Then I found a poster with Steve Belson's picture. He looked like a big, serious, mustached Irish-American. I touched his picture and whispered, "I'm going to tell your story."

I needed to see Ground Zero proper. Security was intense. Not even the press people with media credentials were allowed to go in. I tried to get into nearby buildings to get a look but they were all buttoned down tight. I really hadn't slept for a few days. I felt a little detached from my body. Something I can't explain was coming over me. I continued my walk and came to Murray Street. Here I saw perhaps the most destruction I had seen, up to that point.

Tension in the air was high. The day before, the police had to stop the firemen from searching for victims. It was a brawl. Firemen were arrested, and police were injured. Mayor Giuliani had decided that only 25 police and 25 firemen would be allowed to go on searching. He cited safety reasons and believed it was time to use bulldozers and begin the real cleaning.

I looked up and saw a huge diesel truck that had a container on it. The diesel was parked up on a ramp. The container towered above the barricade. Lifelong surfers are generally pretty good climbers. We scurry up and down slippery cliffs to find good reefs. I saw a clean line going up to that container that was right out of *Rock and Ice* magazine.

There was a cement trash can next to a full-sized work truck. The work truck was by some scaffolding that surrounded that area. Next to the scaffolding, up on a ramp, was the container truck. I looked around and was surprised that there were no police in sight. I set the light reading on my borrowed camera and adjusted my lens for distance. I thought I'd take a picture to show my students. Then I climbed on up. I looked down once; I knew if I fell, it wouldn't be good. I had to jump about five feet from the unstable scaffolding to the top of the container truck. I pulled out the small, chrome ready arm of the camera and made the jump; my landing was a bit rough.

I stood up with a full view. I felt as though I had the breath knocked out of me. My body went slack, and the acrid wind tore at my face. I was hit with a wave of dizziness that made me take a step back. Tens of thousands of pieces of paper whipped upwards in powerful mini-tornadoes. The men working were dwarfed by the jagged carnage. Here was our Hiroshima. Then a roaring woman's voice boomed out. "HE'S ON THE ROOF, HE'S ON THE ROOF!" I snapped out of my stupor and clicked two quick pictures. Down I went.

When I got to the bottom, a news guy and his cameraman were filming me. The news guy asked me if I got the shot.

I said, "I think so." I walked off away from the perimeter. I saw a dark bar and thought about darting in, going into the bathroom, and changing my clothes and hiding my camera. But it's been quite a few years since I've run from the police, so I just walked fast. In my mind I really thought I was home free. I kept thinking, "I got a shot for the kids, I got a shot for the kids." I was just about to round the corner to freedom when I heard a man shout, "Freeze! You fucking freeze right there!"

I used to work with a guy who became a cop.

He told me, "If you're ever in trouble with the law make sure they can see your hands." I held the camera out with both hands and watched the cop sprint towards me. He had out his black club in a combative position. He wore a flak vest, and in New York all the police have medals of some sort or another. This cop had a slew of them. His name was Officer Valverde. His red face was twisted in anger and sweat flew off the tip of his nose. It all felt surreal and dream-like.

"You're under arrest. I'm arresting you. You have

the right to remain silent. Anything you say can and will be used against you in a court of law. You have the right to an attorney. If you cannot afford one, one will be provided for you. Do you understand your rights?"

He tore the camera out of my hands and frantically tried to rip the film out. It's hard to open the film latch under the best of conditions, and he was getting frustrated.

I thought he might just slam the camera to the ground, so I said, "Please don't destroy the camera, my school loaned it to me." Then thankfully the latch opened, and he tore out the film.

Going to Mexico all my life I've seen a lot of big switchblades. But I've never seen one like his. The blade was at least ten inches long and thick like a hunting knife. It opened so quickly I didn't even see it. He started hacking the film up into smaller and smaller pieces, never taking his eyes off of me. People were gathered across the street to see what was going on. Other police were gathering around us. I still felt disconnected from the whole thing as if it were happening to someone else. I weigh 210 pounds. Officer Valverde lifted me off the ground in a one-armed vice-grip and said, "We're going to the F.B.I."

Then I remembered I hadn't called my daughter yet. Something deep inside me began to stir.

I said, "I worked seven weeks to get here. I teach U.S. History in San Diego."

He replied, "What if you would have fallen? Did you think of that? What if you would have landed on someone? Did you think of that? This area is my beat and you're going in." I couldn't believe how strong his grip was.

I started to sense a sort of anger rising from within me.

I told him, "Every U.S. History teacher in America should see this. Our enemies teach their children to hate us

Zen 198

from the time they're old enough to learn. We need to teach our students what this blind hatred looks like." With my free hand I pulled out my Southwest High identification that I had in my pocket for just such an occasion. He glanced at it as we walked.

He said, "Mr. Gutierrez, you are under arrest." But his grip loosened enough for me to walk on my own two feet. I thought maybe I was getting through.

I continued, "Officer Valverde, where are the other U.S. History teachers? Why aren't they here? Can you please answer me that? Didn't you ever have a teacher that made a difference in your life?" I knew that a New York cop wouldn't have his mind changed easily, but I needed to call my daughter, not end up in jail.

By now my voice was near yelling and again I repeated, "Officer Valverde, did you ever have a teacher that made a difference in your life? Come on, didn't you have even one? I'm just trying to be a good teacher!" Then he released me, and we abruptly stopped walking. He snapped his head towards me and looked into my eyes for the first time. I knew then he understood. All the wrinkles went out of his face. Tears were running down his cheeks. Salty drops were drifting down my face, too, though I wasn't sure why.

He said in a strong but shaky voice, "Yes, Mr. Gutierrez, I did have a teacher that made a difference in my life. That's why I'm here. I know people need to see this. You can go now."

Somewhat dazed, I walked off. I put the camera deep in my backpack. I called my daughter and told her that everything was fine and I'd call again that night.

I came upon a procession of people wearing red hard hats. A fireman with tears cleaning a path down his dusty face stood next to me.

He said, "They have family in there." I stopped so

they could pass through a massive barricade into Ground Zero itself. The procession all gazed into space. They were someplace far away, in another time.

I headed to Bouley Bakery to see what work they needed me to do. For the next three days this would be my home away from home. For ten hours I unloaded fish, cut fish, then helped cook it. I also cut vegetables. There were people from all over America from all walks of life. I was astounded at the quantity of food we were preparing. We finished at midnight and sat around and talked until 1:30 a.m. I got to my Off Soho Hotel around 2:00 a.m. They should have called the hotel Off Off Soho. I didn't sleep. I just lay in bed and tried to keep my eyes closed.

November 4:

I got up at 6:00 a.m. for my 7:00 a.m. shift. I started walking to save cab fare, but some shady characters were sniffing an easy mark. I jumped in a cab. I was going to work until 1:00 p.m. Then I was meeting some friends of Fire Fighter Belson at Ladder 24 station.

There was some heavy lifting to do at Bouley's so they asked a man named Goodman and me to help. Goodman is a forester, a bear of a man who crunches numbers in the Federal Building. Like me, he's quiet, so we got along well. All morning we schlepped cases of frozen turkey around, unloaded produce, carried out the big red food containers, and delivered supplies among the labyrinthine network of kitchens.

Late in our shift I asked him what it was like September 11th.

I could barely hear his soft reply as he looked into the sky. "I don't know. I just don't know. We evacuated. Then I just stood and watched. I didn't know the first tower had fallen. I thought it was just smoke. Then I saw that the tower was gone. It was just gone. So now I come here and work. And every day I work it adds another memory."

Zen 200

I took a cab to fire station Ladder 24 on West 31st Street. My cab driver was a Sikh from India. He wore a turban, and I asked him if people realized that he was from India.

In a beautiful singsong voice, he told me, "When I leave the city, people throw baseball bats and bottles at my car. So now me, and my family stay here in the city where people are educated. For two weeks after the terrible day, all the Sikh taxi drivers drove people who needed help anywhere they needed to go for free. Anywhere! I spend more time on these streets than I do with my family. I've gone to those towers almost every day for the last 15 years. I loved those towers, and I love this city. Now we must educate the people."

The fire fighters were expecting me, and I was humbled by their kindness. They took me back to where the firemen lived between calls. Brian Thomas was my main contact. He was wrapping up a stuffed puppy in a box to mail out.

Another fireman grabbed a letter off the table and said, "Listen to this," then read, "Dear Firemen, I've been saving my money a long time for a puppy. I have $11.00. I want to give it to you so I can help. I also cut out an outline of my hand. Just in case someone needs one to hold."

We sat around. Most of these guys smoked pretty hard. I figured it was part of their training. I asked if any female fire fighters were lost. One fireman replied, "No women were lost. We fight high-rise fires down here. There's only one woman who ever passed the test. She's the only woman working down here, but she passed the same test I passed. She can hold her own. Otherwise it's all men."

Steve Belson's last known position was the lobby of the World Trade Center. The N.Y. Fire Department was his

Zen 201

whole life. He was a fire fighter for 22 of his 51 years. He was born in Queens and attended Francis Lewis High School. He graduated from Lehman College in the Bronx with a degree in physical education and worked for several years as a lifeguard before becoming a fireman. Steve would come to work early so he could swim in the 42nd Street pool, where he logged in hours of laps. As the firemen spoke about Steve, they started laughing. They agreed that he was pretty grumpy up until the last year of his life, when he met Josephine. It seemed Josephine had turned Steve into a very content man. Then we all laughed together, understanding that a man is only truly happy when he is getting some regular loving. Every spot has its King. Bells was the King of 92nd Street, the last jetty of Rockaway Beach. He was a fixture there. Bells rented there until he could afford to buy. Recently the City Council changed the name of 92nd Street to Bells' Beach. His love affair with surfing was true. Steve had made at least a dozen cross-country drives to surf his favorite California break, Blacks. He also frequented Puerto Rico where he loved the Rincon area and Sandy Beach. He and his buddies grew up doing road trips to Cape Hatteras, where Steve once was chased in double-time by a sizable shark. Steve had a collection of ten boards, among them a Hobie, a Dennis Farrell-Dakota Brand, a Plastic Fantastic, an Eastern, and a Challenger. They went to his friends and to some local kids who needed boards.

Steve's lifelong friend, Chief John McGuire, got Steve's coveted Challenger Surfboard. I spoke to Chief McGuire over the phone. He said, "Steve was my best friend. We surfed for 30 years together, but he didn't rip. A head dip became a stand-up barrel." The chief had joy in his voice as he continued, "Steve would lie about size of waves like crazy. Oh, he exaggerated the size of the waves big time. But we're not kids anymore. Steve just loved being on the ocean. Surfing was his passion. He was the mayor of Rockaway Beach. I miss him."

Steve was so dedicated to his station that they called him "Mr. Ladder 24." He chose to remain a fire fighter as opposed to moving up the ranks. A friend, Kevin Callaghan, said, "Steve was brave every day. He was one of the most senior and knowledgeable fire fighters at Ladder 24." Steve also loved to ski. Brian Thomas remembered one night flying into Vail with Steve, ready to go out and party.

Steve told Brian, "We've got to get some sleep so we can ski hard!" In the early morning darkness, Brian woke to see Steve fully dressed in his ski clothes, smoking a cigarette and looking out the window. I started to realize that these men lived to touch the sun, save lives, and come back again. But there were no guarantees. Steve's friend and musician Jack Pati wrote a song for Steve. I like the feeling of the following verse:

Bells loved his Rock and Roll
The Dead, Hot Tuna and the like
He was happy cause he followed his dream
And was able to live his own life
He didn't waste a minute a day
Doing things he didn't want to do
And saying things he didn't want to say
It just wasn't Bells' way.

Then the firemen spoke of Mayor Giuliani's decision to bring in the bulldozers. One fireman said, "Fucking Giuliani, America's mayor. What a bunch of shit. What a politician. Why is he in Arizona for the Series? Why didn't he give his tickets to some kids whose dads aren't coming home?" It's not easy to watch men suffer, but this fireman was in the worst kind of pain. He quietly asked me, "What if someone you loved was in there? What would you do? Really, what would you do? My family is in there. So many people have family in there. What do we say to the kids? 'Oh, we can't find your father.' Giuliani said we were going to get them all out. He said we wouldn't stop until they were all out. What happened to that? If anybody tries to stop me from going in there, I'm knocking them down." I believed him.

It was time for me to leave. The day had turned into night, but I needed the walk back to Bouley's Bakery. Somehow I knew that it wasn't fair that I could walk away from Ladder 24 Station while the fire fighters had to stay, waiting for the next alarm. I realized, of course, they wouldn't have it any other way.

When I returned to Bouley's, it was time to cut vegetables. I unloaded a pallet of onions and brought them in one box at a time. Then I joined the cutters. Onions only hurt your eyes for awhile, then you get used to them. After all the onions were cut, it was time to make limejuice. We cut a carton full of limes in half then squeezed the juice into buckets. Then I cleaned the large red food containers, an endless task. It was midnight, and the shift was done. I knew I couldn't sleep, so I walked towards Ground Zero. The strong smell of marijuana drifted through the Manhattan air. I imagined the police now have more important things to do. I walked around the perimeter for an hour until I thought I might be able to fall asleep. It was very quiet. Then I caught a cab back to the Off Soho Suites. I did a little writing then crawled into bed. I dreamt of an impossibly giant and perfect wave. I was quivering in my anticipation to surf it, only to open my eyes to my sparse hotel room.

November 5:

The phone rang with my 6:00 a.m. wake-up call. I was sore as hell all over. I stumbled to the shower, grateful for the thundering, steaming water. Then I caught a cab back to Bouley's. I spent the day cleaning, draining, prepping, seasoning, racking, and finally cooking 42 turkeys. I tasted the finished product, and it wasn't bad. Then I helped load Red Cross trucks and took a shift standing guard over the waiting food. One of the chefs estimated that Bouley's kitchen had produced over 800,000 worker-meals. How it works is the Red Cross drivers tell us what they need and then we load their trucks. More than anything the Ground Zero workers seem to need protein. Temperature control is vital for the safety of the food. One chef told me, under the condition of anonymity, that there were 800 cases of food poisoning at the Oklahoma City bombing and that they couldn't let that happen here. Any food not eaten got thrown out.

I felt bad throwing out so much food, but the chef said, "That's the way it is. You'll get used to it."

Many of the chefs at Ground Zero have flown in on their own dime. They've been working 110 to 130 hours a week since the tragedy. They pay for their own hotels. If you've worked in a fine dining restaurant, you know that the chef is emperor. Bring together many major chefs into one kitchen, and you would normally see egos collide. Not here. There is a hierarchy, and there's no bickering in the ranks. Everyone quietly does his or her job. After working alongside the chefs for three days it was easy to talk to them.

I was working with a chef named Harold, who I asked about September 11th.

He said, "I was in my apartment overlooking the World Trade Center, when I felt my building shake. I turned on the TV and watched. Unfuckingbelievable. Then the second plane hit, and my power went out. I went outside and looked up. At first I couldn't understand what I was seeing. I don't even know how many people I saw jumping out of windows. A man's shirt flew up over his head, and people were trying to swim in the air. Another man had his shirt off, but I looked away before he hit the ground. After a minute I stopped looking. The Tower started coming down, and I still couldn't move. Then a huge piece of the tower hit the pavement, and I felt the ground move under my feet. That snapped me out of it and, for the first time ever I was running for my life. My heart goes out to all those who lost loved ones. But the truth is, there's nothing left in there. They're gone. It's time to clean it up and get this city back on its feet. Giuliani is right; it's time to bring this area back to life. He's making a tough decision, but look around, we're dying here."

I worked until 3:00 p.m. Then I took my last walk around the perimeter. There were work crews deep in the streets around Ground Zero, hundreds and hundreds of men and women working in the trenches. I spoke to a supervisor and asked him what kind of hours they were working: twelve-hour days, seven days a week. All the digging must be done by hand. Many of the main water pipes were laid in the 1860s. There are no blueprints, and hundreds of pipes go every which way. Sewer and steam pipes from Con Ed, water, electricity, and gas. Like a wound on a body, this is how Ground Zero will heal, from the edges inward.

I've heard many people say we'll never be the same. After Pearl Harbor, men slept on the beaches of San Diego awaiting the predicted Japanese invasion. Sometimes they had nothing more than a pick or shovel for a weapon. But these Americans wanted to be there to protect their families and country. The nation will heal. The question remains: Will we ever be the same?

My plane left J.F.K. at 8:00 p.m. for Ontario, California. I drove into my driveway at 3:00 a.m.

I went to my wife and she squeezed me tightly, telling me, "I'm so glad you're home, I love you." Then I went and kissed my sleeping children. I went downstairs and sat on my rocking chair. Our German Shepherd, Aja, nuzzled against my leg. Now that I knew my family was safe, I wanted to drive back to the airport and get on a plane for New York. What if the produce truck needed unloading? What if some meat needed delivering? What if some fish needed cleaning?

November 11:
It's Veteran's Day morning. I'm in my classroom and there are no students. I came in to finish this article and overnight it to Steve Pezman at *The Surfer's Journal*. There is an e-mail from a friend in Manhattan. It says, "A plane just crashed into Queens. Over 250 on board. They're saying mechanical failure. The city is completely shut down. I can hear military jets flying overhead and sirens down on the streets. I'm pretty numbed up. How much more? Pray for us."

I Miss You

On the night Teri called me and told me the Navy had found your empty boat, I could not sleep. In the quiet of the shadows, I walked to the water's edge. I sat looking at the sea and the stars through my tears.

I asked aloud, "God, please give me a sign." On the dark sea a green light glowed. It was brilliant and brief. I knew then that I would never give up hope.

Later the Coast Guard towed your boat back to Honolulu. I collected all your charts and books. I pored over them looking for a note from you. Through the pages of Dostoyevsky, Wilde, and Tennyson, I searched to no avail. Now our son Tiger is older, and he is smitten with your maps. He loves to spread them all over the floor and hear stories about his Uncle Earl.

Zen 208

I'm waiting for you to come and knock on my door. When you do, I'll say, "I knew you were alive! I've kept all your books and charts for you. Earl, Earl, the black pearl."

The author wishes to thank: Jesus Christ, Beanie, Stormy, Tiger, Mom and Dad, my Grandparents, Mark Foreman and North Coast Calvary Chapel, Paseo Del Rey Church, Mariel Hemingway, all the guys at Sunset Cliffs, the Pope family, Sorans, Baby Brim and family, Rocky and family, Roger and Judi, Steve and Debbee Pezman, E.J., Skip and Donna Frye, Steve Belson NYFD, Ed Zieralski, Big Sid, Tiffany Cherwick, Julia and the boys, Pierces, Estes family, Shays, Carlitos, Danny and Gregory, Nine, Deke, Tree, D.C., Loren Nancarrow, Kurty and family, Brad and Jenny, P.T., Steel, Nippy, Dr. Borkat, Dr. Jackson Benson, Dr. Polkinhorn, Dr. Nerricio, Dr. Latta, Sean Collins, Taco Surf, Ken Blanchard and family, Richard Tong, San Diego State University, County of San Diego, City of Mammoth Lakes, City of Carlsbad, Sweetwater Unified High School District, S.D.S.A., Dave McCoy, Mammoth Mountain Ski Association, Farenheit 451 Book Store, and the State of Hawaii. And, of course: Mikey, Kaight, Pedro, Tara, LaRon, Torchea and Radar, see you on the other side.

To order a copy of *Zen and the Art of Surfing*, go to www.greggutierrez.com
or
www.amazon.com

Greg Gutierrez teaches English at Chula Vista High School of Creative and Performing Arts, a very fine school indeed.

Coming soon
Mammoth Mountain
A Novel
By Greg Gutierrez